THE C

"Oh, I have wanted you so!"

THE
CINDERELLA GIRL

E M Channon

Illustrated by
R. F. C. WAUDBY

Books to Treasure

Books to Treasure
5 Woodview Terrace,
Nailsea, Bristol, BS48 1AT
UK

www.bookstotreasure.co.uk
www.facebook.com/BooksToTreasure

First published by Thomas Nelson & Sons 1937
This edition 2016

Design and layout © Books to Treasure

ISBN 978-1-909423-52-7

CONTENTS

PREFACE

E M Channon was born Ethel Mary Bredin on 17 October 1875 in Ireland. After her father's death four years later, she and her mother moved to St Leonard's where she attended the Ladies' College. She married Rev Francis Channon in 1904 and together they had six children. Ethel began writing after her marriage and produced numerous books for both children and adults. She is, perhaps, best known for *The Honour of the House*, which was published in 1931, but she wrote another dozen or so stories for girls between 1924 and 1937. She died on 6 June 1941.

THE CINDERELLA GIRL

CHAPTER I

The Last Speech Day

ONE school Speech Day is very like another. The girls are nervous in uniform, or in white frocks, according to school custom; and the headmistress is probably quite as nervous in her cap and gown, though she hides it much better. Every father present thinks his girl the most attractive of the lot: every mother knows that hers deserves more prizes than any other. The speakers on the platform are more or less bored by every speech except their own, and the audience is bored by them all. On one point only every one is fully agreed—a most hearty thankfulness when it is all over.

Stacy Wayland, sitting among the hefty ranks of VI*b*, was perhaps as well content as any person in the hall. She had no anxiety about prizes, because she knew that she was not going to get any. This was her last Speech Day at St. Alkmund's, and therefore, from a slightly sentimental point of view, more tolerable than any of its predecessors. She was not singing in any of the choruses, having reduced Miss Scales, the music-mistress, almost to tears by her singular lack of ear. She was well placed for seeing things in general, which didn't matter so very much; and in particular for seeing Agatha Phayre go up to take the many prizes that would undoubtedly fall to her lot—and that mattered a great deal, for Stacy adored Agatha with all her extremely warm heart. The only fly in her ointment, in fact, was the presence immediately behind her, in the more exalted ranks of VI*a*, of Janet Tripp. It was annoying to think that Janet, like (but how unlike!) Agatha, would undoubtedly get prizes; it was much worse to know that she would keep up a running commentary, in that clever way of hers that no mistress ever overheard, on all that went on during the afternoon. Yes, there she was, at it already!

"Stacy!"

"Um?" Stacy returned discouragingly without turning round.

"Sue Custance has got mumps. *Isn't* she unlucky?"

"Oh, *bad* luck!" Stacy returned, roused against her will.

"A good thing that she's a day-girl," said Janet callously. "I say! Did you see that the button came off Miss Trumpet's shoe as she went up to the platform? ... Do you think Margery Pargeter will stick it out this afternoon? She looks awfully white; and she's fainted *three* times at Speech Days! ... My father says that the Bishop is the dullest speaker he's ever heard in his life. Isn't it *grim*?"

Stacy stared in front of her. If she could keep on doing that, without again being betrayed into any expression of interest, Janet might—just possibly—turn her attention and her comments elsewhere.

But …

"I say!" came the penetrating murmur once more. And once more, still more reluctantly, Stacy repeated:

"Um?"

"Do you see the very tall man at the end of the fourth row?"

"Um!"

"Do you know who that is?"

Stacy shook her head, not vouchsafing any sound at all.

"It's Sir Humphrey Phayre!"

"It *isn't*!" Stacy cried sharply, betrayed once more into interest.

"But it *is*," Janet persisted, delighted at her success. "Agatha's just told me. She's *thrilled*. He didn't expect to get here in time."

Stacy sat staring, with flushed cheeks and a fast-beating heart. Imagine that man being her adored Agatha's adored father, who, like Agatha herself, had everything that Fate could give in his favour! Famous explorer, brilliant speaker, fabulously rich, immensely good-looking, universally popular. No wonder that Agatha was thrilled! Stacy found it thrilling enough even to see such a being. She was hardly conscious of the persistent voice behind her.

"I say! Won't Miss Trumpet be furious not to have got him on the platform! *Isn't* it a pity that she's asked the Bishop! Don't you wish …"

Even Janet's voice was drowned in the general rising of every one present as the undesired Bishop walked in with the Governing Body—a very small Bishop indeed, with a bent white head and the thinnest possible gaiters. From him Stacy's enthralled glance flew back to the tall figure standing at the end of the fourth row, taller by inches than any one near him, standing easily and naturally, like a person well accustomed to being looked at—as every one in his neighbourhood was, not unnaturally, looking. For half a moment Stacy tore her eyes away to glance back at Agatha's enraptured face, full of pride and joy. … It must be nice (thought Stacy, who had no relations there) to have some one like that belonging to you; it must be *very* nice …

An awful silence had fallen. The stiff ceremonies of the afternoon were beginning.

It took a solid hour for the preliminary speeches and most of the singing to be got toilsomely through; and the Bishop was undoubtedly dull beyond words; and Miss Trumpet dropped one sheet of her notes, and it fluttered off the platform and was returned to its scarlet owner, after a most embarrassing interval, by a small visiting child afflicted with hiccups. Then, at long last, the School settled audibly into its places with sighs of relief. There was only the prize-giving now, and that was always jolly well managed and extremely rapid, and anyhow it was interesting; and there was only a very short time, comparatively speaking, to be lived through before one could join one's relations and begin to enjoy oneself. The prize-winners were already forming up in single file, processing statefully down the narrow aisle left between visitors for their use. The babies first, very sweet and solemn and unselfconscious, in spite of audible comments from all sides on their "duckiness." The small children next, shy and unhappy. The Middle School, shyer and more unhappy still, and terribly aware of the length of its legs and the size of its shoes and the redness of its hands. Miss Trumpet's voice, rapidly reading the list, began to grow a little hoarse. The little Bishop, smiling a vague, painstaking smile, shook hands conscientiously still with each prize-winner, but he had long ago given up his original well-meaning attempt to say "a few words" as a running accompaniment to the books.

Miss Trumpet cleared her throat and announced:

"Form VI*b*."

Bother! Stacy knew that she had no prize to get, but she had quite forgotten that wretched certificate. She hurried hastily out of her place to join the throng in single file; and she heard her thrice-hated name read aloud for all to hear, and she stumbled going up the platform steps; and the Bishop's little claw of a hand was unpleasantly cold and limp; and she felt Miss Trumpet's eye upon her—especially upon the safety-pin that was replacing a dud snap just below her collar. And going back, clutching her certificate, she met point-blank the eye of the tall man who sat at the end of the fourth row. She had never seen any glance so piercing, so amused—he saw the safety-pin all right, even though he was a mere man—so brilliantly blue.

"You nearly forgot to go up, didn't you?" Janet murmured penetratingly into her ear as she sat down again.

Stacy didn't attempt to answer. Now, at least, she was free from all further chance of uprooting! The ordeal had, fortunately, been unexpected, and therefore robbed of half its terrors; and it was over, and over for good.

"Form VI*a*," said Miss Trumpet, undeniably very hoarse now.

Stacy leaned eagerly forward, for this was the moment for which she had all along been waiting. Her glance slid contemptuously away from Janet (very cockahoop and self-conscious) to Agatha just behind her: so fair and tall and graceful, so obviously popular, so surprisingly (considering her advantages) shy and nervous. Any success always seemed to surprise Agatha, though one might have thought that by this time she would have become accustomed to them. She appeared to be quite genuinely unaware of her good looks. She went up to receive her three prizes—meeting on the steps Janet swanking vaingloriously down with her two—as blushing and modest as if she had never done such a thing before. The

applause was tremendous—no one could doubt that she was
a popular person. Miss Trumpet beamed graciously at her—
any one could see what a credit she was to the school. Even
the Bishop pulled himself together, looked quite human as he
shook hands, and murmured some pretty nothing that made
Agatha blush more becomingly than ever. But she had no eyes
for him, or for Miss Trumpet, or for any of her schoolfellows:
only for the tall man who was clapping like mad at the end of
the fourth row. … Yes. Stacy found a sudden odd little catch
in her throat as she thought again that it must be pleasant to
have a father like that.

Stacy leaned eagerly forward.

Agatha was back again among VI*a*, in a flurry of whispered congratulations and patting hands and murmured inquiries as to the nature of the books. Stacy (who was only in VI*b*) was not, of course, among these commentators; she contented herself with turning from her inferior position and beaming satisfaction. It was like Agatha, who, for all her modesty, could not well fail to be aware of such very notable hero-worship, to lean over from the exalted ranks behind and show Stacy what her three books were. That was indeed a heartening privilege.

"H'sh-sh-sh!"

"It is our custom," Miss Trumpet was saying in her usual final phrase, after a good deal of throat clearing, "to end our prize-giving by the presentation of the School Prize. For the information of those who have not been with us before, I may explain that it is a prize given by the vote of the whole School— each girl having her vote—to the girl who is considered most useful to the School. This year," she smiled, "the voting has been extraordinarily even, and the winner is only first by two votes."

Stacy, staring with a righteous indignation, was furious. The prize, of course, was Agatha's; there could be no two opinions about that. But who could possibly have been the runner-up? Margaret Blaise? But Margaret, though frightfully clever, was a perfect dud at games. Barbara Potter? But Barbara, though frightfully good at games, was a perfect dud at lessons. Mildred Crawford, though good at both, had such a vile temper that every one hated her. Every one liked Phoebe Taylor; but she couldn't really be considered *useful* to the School—she was so much too ready to do whatever anybody wanted, whether it was desirable or not. Lesley Drabble had been simply splendid with the Guides; but then, she had left last term. … A little excited, affected cough just behind made Stacy turn and glare with additional fury. How *like* Janet to imagine that she had the ghost of a chance! She had two prizes, of course, and she was a good tennis player and really very good at lax, and she was a keen Guide. But surely nobody in the School would waste a vote on a person whose chief gift was rubbing everybody, mistresses and girls alike, the wrong way!

"The winner of the School Prize," said Miss Trumpet, trying very hard to get her voice clear for this final and most important announcement, "is Anastasia Wayland."

There was a loud singing in Stacy's ears—she *couldn't* have heard aright! It was quite out of the question, a thing never dreamed of—she, Stacy Wayland, only in VI*b*, nothing very special at games, always being dropped on for untidiness. Yet every one was looking at her—it was awful—and Janet was poking her hard from behind and saying, in a very sour and disappointed tone, "Go *on*, you chump!" And then Agatha's soft voice came instantly after: "Stacy, I *am* glad!" And that woke her up, and convinced her at last, and sent her stumbling out of her place and up the central aisle—more conscious than ever of that safety-pin under her left ear.

"I congratulate you, Miss Anastasia, on your prize and on your beautiful name," said the Bishop's little thin voice. And Stacy, who hated her name from the bottom of her soul, thought reprehensibly: "Oh, *lor*!" and clutched her large and magnificent book, and thought again that the Bishop's hand was like a cold thin claw, and hurried back to her place amidst a thunder of clapping. ... The whole thing, of course, was a mistake, and perfectly incomprehensible. ...

"You'll have to come and help with the tea," Janet's acid voice sounded in her ear almost immediately afterwards. "Margery Pargeter's fainted again, *as* usual!"

CHAPTER II

TEA—AND TEA

IT was the unenviable privilege of VI*a* to wait on the visitors, in a small hot room where there was hardly room to move, while happier, less exalted people gladly escaped with their relations to more eligible meals elsewhere. Stacy was not afflicted in this particular respect, as she had no visiting relations for Speech Day; but, for all that, she was far from grateful for her exaltation. She had a rooted conviction that she would drop things, and spill things, and conduct herself generally with a terrible want of success. There was Agatha, of course, gliding gracefully about as if it were the easiest business in the world. There was Miss Trumpet, trying gallantly to pay equal attention to all her guests simultaneously, and other selected mistresses imitating her to the best of their ability. There was the Bishop, sitting very unhappy in a corner, with a cup of tea balanced precariously on his aproned knee. There was Janet Tripp being terribly, blatantly efficient, and letting every one know it.

Stacy made a dive for the food table and secured two plates— nothing spillable for her if she could help it! One of them held rather dry sandwiches, curling up at the corners, and the other was precariously piled with sugary cakes, none of them looking in their first freshness. She couldn't wonder that one person after another declined her offer of these unattractive viands; but it was pretty awful, all the same, to go round getting nothing but refusals. The room seemed to be more crowded every minute—would no one *ever* go? or was it conventional to wait for the Bishop to make the first move, as if he were a bride? He would have to go through the crowds diagonally, of course, like his namesake on the chessboard. … Stacy found herself giggling internally, an affliction which was only too apt to take her unawares, at the most inauspicious moments.

"Miss Anastasia," said a voice high above her head, "will you tell me what is amusing you?"

As Stacy gave a jump and looked up, her plate of sugary cakes tilted sideways and slid away from her; and her wild grab only hastened the catastrophe. In all directions they rolled, among the crowded feet of the guests. Stacy's agonized eye followed a chocolate-covered lump, on which a very nice lizard-skin shoe had just set its unsuspecting heel; a weltering pink mess, already trodden well and truly into the carpet; a doughnut bounding blithesomely away and hitting the Bishop on his gaitered shin. … It was *awful*.

"My fault *entirely*!" said Sir Humphrey Phayre.

His tone showed a very proper regret, but his voice shook suspiciously. … Stacy, looking up again, suddenly gurgled with laughter, and then looked round in agony for the terrible eye of Miss Trumpet.

"It's all right," said Sir Humphrey. "She's talking to an old lady in purple in the far corner. … The room is terribly hot, and I'm not used to this sort of thing. Do you think it would be incorrect for you to give me a sandwich, just outside the door?"

"I'm afraid they look rather beastly," said Stacy, following him.

"I won't eat it," Sir Humphrey promised her seriously.

It was certainly cooler in the passage outside, but Stacy had qualms of conscience that her place was not there.

"Perhaps I ought …" she suggested uncertainly.

"Not at all!" said Sir Humphrey. "I am a perfect stranger here, and some one ought to entertain me; and, as a matter of duty, I think it is dangerous for you to encourage any one to eat these sandwiches—I wouldn't think of doing it myself.

Now tell me why you were so amused on a far from amusing occasion."

"I was thinking about the Bishop's move …" Stacy gurgled again; and he took her meaning in a moment and laughed with her.

"I am quite sure you hate all this as much as I do," he told her. "I am only waiting to get hold of Agatha and escape, Bishop or no Bishop; but she seems in such general request …"

"Oh, she always is!" said Stacy quickly; with a warm pride.

He liked that. She could see it in his answering glance, which was quick and proud too.

"I want to take her out to tea, of course. I suppose you are waiting for your people to do the same?"

Stacy shook her head. "I haven't any one here," she said briefly.

"No relations here? Then, in that case, please come with us."

As he began to speak those delightful words another voice spoke simultaneously:

"Sir Humphrey, you have nothing to eat! … Oh, did you mean me? I have no one here, and I should love to!"

It was Janet Tripp, of course; like Little Mary of the old song, always in the way. She had come dashing up with plates of food, just in time to intercept that heavenly invitation and appropriate it to herself—and even Sir Humphrey appeared to see no way out of it. He said very politely, in a stiff voice quite different from the one that had been talking to Stacy, that that was very kind of her, that he already had a sandwich, thank you; and that, if it were possible to reach Agatha …

The ever-efficient Janet did that in the twinkling of an eye, possibly fearing that if she allowed him to say any more he might in some way free himself from her toils. Like a highly trained sheep-dog she cut Agatha out from the people who were flocking around her, shepherded her to the door, and obviously expected to be taken out then and there, which plan Sir Humphrey, looking a little dazed, put into immediate execution. He had a fine large car outside, and Janet explained that it was quite impossible to get at Miss Trumpet and say good-bye—besides, no one ever did! In three minutes hats and coats were donned and they were off—Janet, needless, to say, sitting beside her host. She was like that.

"Stacy, I am so glad about the School Prize!" said Agatha, as they sat cosily behind in the great billowy seat.

"It's awfully good of you, but there *must* have been some mistake about it!" said Stacy, in obvious discomfort of mind. "Why on earth should *I* have it?"

Agatha laughed her soft and pretty laugh.

"Why, because you are always doing things for other people—the unattractive things that get shirked! Who's run the Brownies all this year, since Evelyn Tupman crocked? You know they simply adore you!"

"Rubbish!" said Stacy, very hot. "They're jolly little things; it doesn't take so very much extra time."

"Yes, it does, as you do it," Agatha insisted mildly. "You're always working out new things for them to do, and you don't mind how much trouble or time you take to teach them anything. ... Then there was all that endless copying out of lists for Miss Selfe when she was ill—Oh, yes, she told me! And that hateful child Maisie Cree would certainly have been expelled if you hadn't taken her in hand ..."

"She'd never had a chance—her people are perfectly *foul* ..."

The car had stopped, not at the cosy Cottage Tea Rooms, much frequented by girls with visiting parents, but at the splendacious Gloriosa Café, with its window banked with superior chocolates and great ribboned boxes set in cushion-like beds of pale pink material. Stacy had never been inside, and showed it by the awe with which she entered. Janet had never been inside, and showed it by her too-obvious carelessness of manner. Agatha took it as a matter of course.

"Now, then!" said Sir Humphrey.

It seemed as if every one in the shop had flown to do his bidding, to find him the best table, to take his orders, not with the haughty indifference suited to such a place, but with an eager humility. He too took it all as a matter of course. Food of the most glorious description was piled up all round them; and what a comfort it is, under similar circumstances, to find that one's host intends to eat quite a lot himself! After school meals it was like a dream of fairyland.

"The last term for all three of you, isn't it?" said Sir Humphrey, eating a large éclair as if he liked it.

They all said "Yes" in varying tones of voice: Agatha with a gentle pleasure, Janet in the superior tone of one who has already escaped from the bondage of being a schoolgirl, Stacy a little doubtfully. She had been happy at St. Alkmund's— much happier during term-time than in the holidays. She would simply hate saying good-bye to all her friends.

"And what," said Sir Humphrey, looking at the two girls who were not his daughters, "are you going to do next?"

Janet was most pleased to tell him. She was going to a Secretarial Training College for a year. After that a good post was waiting for her in the office of a convenient uncle. It was all cut and dried, and efficient, and just like Janet herself. Stacy, when she was given an opportunity to speak—which was not very soon—said that she was going to a Domestic Science College.

"And what do you expect to learn there?" Sir Humphrey inquired.

Stacy, with one of her sudden irrepressible gurgles, said that she thought they learned everything! Cooking, housework, dressmaking, laundry, hygiene—all that sort of thing.

"And how long do they take to teach you all that?"

"Four terms," said Stacy.

"Will you like it?" Sir Humphrey inquired further.

Stacy thought she would. Other girls from St. Alkmund's had gone through a similar training and liked it very much indeed, though they said it was fearfully hard work.

"And when you leave this place of All Knowledge?"

"Oh, then I'll get a job," said Stacy quickly and cheerfully.

"What sort of a job?"

"Well, under somebody at first, of course, to learn how to manage big numbers: cook, or housekeeper, or something like that."

"And will you like it?" Sir Humphrey inquired again. He seemed really interested.

"Oh, yes, I'm sure I shall!" said Stacy still very cheerfully. As a matter of fact, for private reasons, the only thing she dreaded was the possibility of *not* getting a job.

"*I* shall only need a year at my College," Janet here struck in. She had been listening with a rising impatience, rather peeved that no questions were asked about her prospects.

Sir Humphrey listened to her politely, but it was to Stacy that he turned again.

"Well, at any rate you will be in a sound position, whatever comes to the world," he said. "Even if we're under a Soviet government by that time there will always be a need of cooks!"

Janet looked very decidedly annoyed. In common politeness, he might at least have added that any sort of government would of course need secretaries—who are, of course, very much higher in the social scale than mere cooks! But he added nothing of the sort. He was smiling at his own girl, and she was smiling back.

"Well," he said, "while you people are being so busy and growing so learned, I am afraid Agatha and I are going to have a lazy, wandering time together abroad. When we come back, we shall see how you have got on!"

"I shall only need a year at my College."

"Yes," said Janet with considerable complacency. She had not the least doubt in the world how *she* would have got on.

"Yes," said Stacy, but not very clearly because of a sudden lump in her throat. It must be nice to have a father who took one abroad for indefinite months of luxurious travelling. It must be still nicer to be looked at as Sir Humphrey was now looking at Agatha.

He drove them both back to the School, and took Agatha on to dine with him at his hotel. It was well for one of his guests that she could not hear his remarks as the great car glided off.

"When we come home, Agatha, we'll have that Anastasia child to stay with us. What a name!"

"Stacy, Father. She simply hates it."

"No wonder!" said Sir Humphrey, apparently quite disagreeing with the Bishop.

"I should *love* to have her!" said Agatha in her soft impulsive way. "I don't think she is a bit happy at home—I don't know why. She never says anything much about it, but I *don't* think so."

Sir Humphrey swerved suddenly to avoid one of those unforgivable pedestrians who persist in crossing from one side of the road to the other. His voice, when he answered, was slightly savage.

"As for that bumptious young woman who put us all in our places and accepted an invitation that was never meant for her, don't let me ever hear her name again!"

"A NASTASIA!"

"Yes, Aunt Monica?"

"When you have finished stoning the raisins, I wish you would take the children out. The wind is very sharp, and I have a little cold."

"Yes, Aunt Monica."

"But I promised to take them to buy their presents to-day, and they must not be disappointed."

"No, Aunt Monica."

Mrs. Phipps pulled her woollen coat a little closer round her and gave a little cough, to show that the cold was quite genuine, gently closing the door after her.

Well, thank goodness the raisins were nearly done! that sticky, thankless, detestable job which is the worst part of Christmas preparations. It is possible, of course, to buy them ready stoned: but Mrs. Phipps was mildly sure that most of the goodness must be taken out in that process, and quite convinced that it was well worth the trouble to do them in the old-fashioned way. She never did it herself, any more than she ever did the little disagreeable jobs that occur in every household—not refusing to do them, just gently gliding away at the critical moment for some quite plausible reason. The pudding raisins were always left until Stacy came home from School, because she would certainly not refuse to do them. At that late stage of proceedings you can't possibly bother a busy cook-general with a finicking job of that sort—why, she might give notice! There was always a long, gentle, wandering explanation why the puddings had not been made, like other people's, weeks before. Stacy had given up listening to that, because it was the same every year.

"Oh—Anastasia!"

What on earth did Aunt Monica want *now*? Stacy turned round from the sink, where she was washing her glutinous fingers.

"I forgot—your Uncle Paul wants you to go to him, in the office, at half-past five."

Now that *was* something new; and Stacy had learnt to distrust novelties. However, there was, of course, only one answer to give.

"Very well, Aunt Monica."

The door did not close this time, because Stacy was quite evidently just ready to leave the kitchen. She listened, drying her hands on the roller towel, to the slow, soft footsteps trailing away in the distance. Then she went and put on her hat and coat and called the children: Howard, eight, who was a prig, and Mona, six, who was a whiner. Mrs. Phipps would have been extremely hurt and surprised if she had known that her children were the reason of Stacy's firmly refusing to take to Froebel work when she was making choice of her future career.

"I am ready and waiting, Anastasia," Howard informed her reprovingly.

"Don't *want* to go out!" Mona fretted. "Nasty cold wind; and I've got a cold!"

"Don't you want to buy your presents?" said Stacy a little wearily—she was so well used to this sort of preliminary.

"It is her duty, whether she wants to or not," said Howard virtuously. "I *want* to go. I like to think of the pleasure that I shall give. Mona is a naughty girl."

"I *not* a naughty girl!" Mona contradicted him with tears.

"You are."

"I *not*!"

"You *are*. You almost always are."

"I *not*! Ow—ow!"

After this pleasant gambit, they bickered all down the length of the road, while Stacy, whose school coat was three years old and rather tight and short, shivered in the wind, and thought how wise her Aunt Monica had been to stay at home. Holidays were always a good deal like this, of course; but now she had begun them in a rather gloomy frame of mind, having said a final good-bye to her school, and hated doing so exceedingly. The present was decidedly bleak. The unknown future looked grey.

They bickered all down the length of the road.

All shops were, of course, full and busy. The children had a strictly limited amount to spend, and Mona never knew her own mind for two minutes together. When it was finally driven into her understanding that ninepence-halfpenny would not buy a large rocking-horse, she wailed aloud. People turned round and stared—feeling, Stacy knew, that she was to blame. Howard (who, to do him justice, had sallied forth with a business-like list and had given little trouble over his purchases) looked on, superior.

"She *is* a naughty girl, isn't she?" he appealed to Stacy.

"I not!" Mona wept afresh.

Stacy led her firmly away from the neighbourhood of the rocking-horse to a counter filled with the small things of the world, saw to it that the ninepence-halfpenny was all laid out as rapidly as possible, and led her charges away, her head defiantly high and her cheeks very red. She heard more than one murmured accusation of "*unkind* to her little sister." She knew, with shame, that the shop-assistants breathed deep breaths of relief as she finally closed the door.

"Nasty wind!" Mona wailed.

"Where's your hanky, Mona?" Stacy inquired with a callous firmness; was told, of course, that Mona "hadn't got none," and reluctantly lent her own for a pressing need. The short walk home was all too long—and what did "Uncle Paul" want in the office at half-past five? ... Not that Stacy ever had called him "Uncle," or ever would: he was, thank heaven! no uncle of hers. "Uncle," in her mind, was dear Uncle Lance: so kind, so jolly, so everything that a relation should be—though, of course, even he was only an uncle by marriage. She had lived with him and darling Aunt Madge ever since her father and mother, whom she barely remembered, had died; and they had been the happiest of little households. And then had come that terrible influenza epidemic which had carried off Aunt Madge after three days' illness, while Uncle Lance and Stacy herself were still too ill to realize very clearly what was happening. And then there had been a grey interval of housekeepers and governess-people, all more or less unattractive and inefficient; and then had come the most terrible blow of all—Uncle Lance had married Aunt Monica. Stacy would never, never understand how he came to do it.

The little house, that had once been so gay, was gay no longer. Instead of bright Aunt Madge, so pretty and sparkling, with her bright eyes and sweet laugh and charming ways, Aunt Monica trailed dimly about, housekeeping rather badly, never really laughing at all, just crushing out, in a mild and gentle way, all the happiness that might have been. There seemed no particular reason why Uncle Lance should have died after two years of it. Stacy had a horrid suspicion that he just didn't care to live any longer.

There must, presumably, have been something queerly attractive about Aunt Monica where men were concerned, for she married Mr. Phipps—never, never Uncle Paul!—before another year had passed. And Stacy became a member of his grim household, being duly given to understand that she ought to think herself a very fortunate girl—for she was, of course, no real relation to any one. And she had been sent to school, learning at once to prefer term-time to the holidays. And first there was Howard, a solemn, ugly, fat baby; and then there was Monica, a whining, pining, skinny baby, whom Howard resented with an immense resentment. And now Stacy had left school and was going to learn to earn her own living—and "Uncle Paul" wanted her in the office at half-past five.

Unlike most solicitors, Mr. Phipps had his office in his own house; and, like the offices of all solicitors, it was a pretty grim place. There were ranges of black tin boxes, each with somebody's name written on it in white paint. There were heavy solemn law-books on bleak black-painted shelves. There was a large forbidding desk and a leather-seated armchair in front of it, turning on a swivel; and another leather chair without arms opposite, facing the window—a tall narrow window, heavily curtained, looking out on to the side wall of the next house. You couldn't imagine any pleasant business being transacted in that room. It was just the place where bitter old aunts would sign wills that cut off their nephews with a shilling, and unfortunate widows would learn that all their money had been lost in gold-mines that never existed.

At half-past five to the moment Stacy knocked at the door of this unpleasing room, was duly bidden to enter, and did so with her heart in her mouth. What on earth did Mr. Phipps (who very rarely spoke to her at all) want of her now?

"Ah, Anastasia! Sit down."

It was not the least of Stacy's counts against him that it was he who had firmly decreed the use of her detested full name at all times. He didn't approve of names being shortened—or of many other things. She sat down and looked at him squarely: at his lank black hair, and his lustreless black eyes, and his blue chin, and his perfectly hideous black-and-white tie.

"Now that you have finally left school, Anastasia, I think it best to have a business talk with you."

"Yes!" said Stacy.

Mr. Phipps leaned back in his swivel chair, put the tips of his fingers together, and looked at her with his black eyes; and Stacy thought, for the thousandth time, that he was exactly her idea of Mr. Murdstone in *David Copperfield*.

"You are now eighteen years old, and quite sufficiently mature to understand your position. … You are probably aware that your late father left only a comparatively small sum of money when he died."

Stacy didn't contradict, though she had not been aware of anything of the kind—it had never occurred to her to think about it.

"Your late uncle, Mr. Lancelot Thorpe, appears to have

kept this small sum untouched, though you lived in his house for some years: a very generous proceeding," said Mr. Phipps in a tone that combined surprise and disparagement. (Stacy didn't answer, because she couldn't. *Dear* Uncle Lance! It would be exactly the sort of thing that he would do, quite naturally, without mentioning it to any one.) "When, however, you came to live with me, things were on a different footing."

Stacy winked away the tears that had risen to her eyes, and said: "Yes. Of course they would be!"

Mr. Phipps eyed her a little doubtfully. His tone, when he went on, was drier and even less friendly.

"As you say—of course they would be. Having been kept at compound interest, the small sum was slightly increased; and I have managed, with care, not only to make it last out through your schooldays, but to retain enough for this course of Domestic Science training upon which you are now about to enter. What I wish you to understand, however, Anastasia, is—that I have only done this by dint of great care and good management, and that at the end of your training it will be finally exhausted."

He made an intentional pause, and Stacy felt morally certain that he expected gratitude for his good stewardship—and she simply couldn't find a word to say. She hadn't the least doubt that he really had done as well as it was possible to do, or the least suspicion that he had defrauded her of a farthing—he wasn't the sort of man that you could suspect of anything but perfect uprightness. But, also, he wasn't the sort of man for whom you could possibly feel anything as warm as gratitude. A sort of chilly respect was the utmost she could bring herself to acknowledge.

Having made his little pause without any response, Mr. Phipps went on in a tone that was definitely soured.

"Do you understand what I mean? At the end of your training you will have no private means left whatever. But, as by that time you will, I believe, be qualified to take a post at a minimum of fifty pounds a year, you should be in no difficulty."

It seemed an enormous sum to Stacy, whose pocket-money had been very strictly limited. She said cheerfully: "Oh, yes, of course! That will be absolutely all right, I'm sure!"

Mr. Phipps appeared to be very slightly embarrassed. He coughed a little dry cough—exactly as solicitors do in books— and hesitated for a moment before saying anything more.

"I am not sure that you *do* exactly understand. That seems to you, I have no doubt, unlimited wealth!" He gave a very little frosty smile. "But I am afraid you will hardly find it so in practice. You have to remember that you will have holidays to consider."

For the moment he did not meet Stacy's wide-eyed gaze. He took up a ruler from his desk and played a little tuneless tattoo with it.

"I have already explained to you that the small inheritance left by your father has just been made to stretch over your expenses until next Easter year—including, of course, your College vacations, which you will naturally spend here, as you have always done. After that period you—will be an independent young woman, Anastasia. We shall always be glad, of course, to see you here occasionally—for Christmas, let us say"—"Yes, to stone raisins for the puddings!" Stacy said furiously to herself—"and for, say, a fortnight in the summer; and naturally we shall always take a sincere interest in your welfare."

"Thank you!" said Stacy, and stood up as if she had been released from a spring. Mr. Phipps looked at her a little doubtfully.

"I think there is nothing else to explain," he said. "You do understand?"

"*Quite*, thank you!" said Stacy, and was out of the room

before the tears, that had rushed to her eyes, had time to fall and disgrace her.

She didn't really know why she was crying—except that it was rather a forlorn prospect to have no sort of place to go to in her future holidays. She had, of course, always hated living in the Phipps's household; she just tolerated Aunt Monica, but the rest of them she frankly disliked. She had a fierce, miserable conviction that she had no cause for gratitude to any one. It was, of course, good of Mr. Phipps to have given her

"I think there is nothing else to explain."

board and lodging, and managed these money affairs of which she had never previously heard; but she had the shrewdest possible idea that all her expenses, down to the uttermost farthing, had been well and truly paid out of her father's money—with scrupulous fairness, of course. Mr. Phipps would have calculated, with the utmost accuracy, just what she cost them, and then deducted that sum week by week from what remained. … And she hadn't been an idle inmate, either! She had done her full share—perhaps more—of what there was to do, and she had helped with the children, and …

"Two letters for you, Anastasia," said Mrs. Phipps, catching her as she went through the hall like a whirlwind. And Stacy muttered a muffled "Thank you!" and flew on, up to her room, leaving Aunt Monica, she knew, standing down below with a dim, baffled expression of faint resentment. She would have *loved* to know all about those letters. Her little interests were so petty, her life was so empty, that that sort of thing was of the deepest interest to her.

One of the letters was merely a tucked-in Christmas card from Janet Tripp, bearing exactly the five words that are allowable for a halfpenny—Janet all over!

The other was on thin foreign paper; and Stacy tore it open eagerly, for it was from Agatha—and, in the same way, was Agatha all over. The warmest Christmas wishes: the deepest regrets that no Christmas present could be enclosed, on account of difficulties with the Customs—"Father says you would very likely not get it in time, Stacy, darling, and perhaps it might never reach you at all! But I've *got* it! and I do think you'll like it—and I shall post it the moment we get back to England. So I *do* hope you will understand and not mind." Agatha was at Cannes, having the most heavenly time in every possible way. She expected to be away all the winter, but when decent weather came—Sir Humphrey hated the cold—they were coming back to find a house and settle down. "And then,

Stacy, you must be our very first visitor, and stay as long as you possibly can!" And Stacy must write as soon as she got to her College, and tell every single thing about it. And Agatha was always her loving friend.

It was a very satisfactory antidote to Mr. Phipps. Stacy, folding it up after reading it all through three times, felt that after all life was not so bleak as she had begun to think it. She was going to College in a fortnight's time, and she was going to work like a nigger, and enjoy herself as much as possible as well. Staying with Agatha would be a perfectly glorious thing to look forward to …

"Anastasia!" called Mrs. Phipps up the stairs.

"Yes, Aunt Monica?"

The glow was gone from Stacy's face: but the letter was safely tucked inside her jumper, to be referred to for comfort at any odd moment when it seemed needed.

"Will you come down and see to the supper? I am putting Mona to bed; and Theodosia has just gone up to her room with a dreadful toothache, and says she can't do any more work to-day."

CHAPTER IV

THE FIRST HOLIDAYS

STRICTLY speaking, they were the second holidays, since measles at Easter had neatly filled up the time between Stacy's finishing one term and beginning another. It wasn't the pleasantest experience in the world; but, on the whole, Stacy hadn't been at all sure that she didn't prefer it to the Phipps' household. And now here was the end of July; and she was escaping from that bleak prospect again, since Agatha had invited her, quite definitely, for "the *whole* of your holidays." Stacy felt a small, grim wonder whether Mr. Phipps might not, after all, find himself compelled to hand over some small sum to her at the end of his stewardship—at the rate of fifteen shillings a week, she reckoned, with her newly acquired knowledge of housekeeping expenses. Possibly, however, those other expenses connected with measles would have eaten up all this surplus.

"Where are you going, Wayland?"

The inquiry came again and again, for Stacy had found her fellow-students a friendly lot; and again and again she gave a glad and full answer, and again and again she was told how jolly lucky she was. And here, at last, the glorious experience was actually beginning, with arrival at a little country station, and finding Agatha waiting outside in a huge blue car, and being greeted with all possible warmth and affection. Stacy's luggage looked pretty dim as it was stored away; but she had been prepared for that, and had sensibly resolved not to mind. Agatha knew that she was poor. Agatha wasn't the sort of person to care twopence how old her suit-case was, and how few and cheap her frocks. Agatha was, in fact, Agatha: not

in the least altered by all these luxurious months of happy
freedom. And Stacy was going to have the time of her life, and
enjoy every minute of it.

"Stacy, you've grown!"

"That was measles," Stacy explained cheerfully, not
displeased to find herself now as tall as Agatha—though
how different in other respects! *She* wasn't slim or graceful or
beautiful. *She* wasn't wearing a frock that had quite evidently
cost ... "*Shut up!*" said Stacy to herself, very severely, and went
on beaming at Agatha as if the forbidden thought had never
entered her head.

"We're a long way from the station, I'm afraid."

"Good!" said Stacy with all her heart. Tired? Rubbish!
And, even if she had been, it was pure joy to drive in a great
luxurious car like this, with Agatha beside her, and the most
perfectly lovely country flitting past the windows. Yes, Agatha
agreed, it *was* a nice part, and she was very glad that they had
fixed on it—they had looked at several other houses first,
scattered about England. Oh, no, Sir Humphrey hadn't *bought*
it! only taken it furnished for the summer. With the first cold
weather he would probably want to be off again, but next year
he really did think of buying a house and settling down for
good. That, Agatha considered, would be lovely ... though, of
course, as Stacy suggested, the last few months of luxurious
wandering had been lovely too. But Sir Humphrey had so
many wonderful things put away, collected during his many
and various travels; and Agatha was simply dying to have them
all out, and look at them, and arrange them in a home of their
own. But their present temporary home was very nice too;
and the people in the neighbourhood were delightful; and the
tennis courts were good ("*Tennis courts!*" thought Stacy with
round eyes); and if only the weather was kind they would have
such fun! The seaside was just near enough to go for a day.
There were all sorts of interesting places to visit, within easy

reach. Did Stacy play billiards? Oh, well, she would have to learn, then! And here they were.

Stacy's eyes grew round again, for they had turned in at imposing gates, with a lodge and a lodge-keeper, and were driving up a long beech avenue with what looked like a young palace at the end of it. There, as Agatha pointed out, were the tennis courts, through the trees, two grass and one hard; and that was quite a jolly swimming pool; and, yes, the rose-garden really was lovely, though one could only see just the edge of it from here. The people who owned the place had made a great feature of it.

Stacy got out, feeling remarkably small, at the foot of a great semi-circular sweep of stone steps; and her absurd impression, as she mounted them, was that she had never in her life seen such absolutely enormous coco-nut mats as the two at the top. She had an awful instantaneous fear that there would be a butler and footmen—terrible in themselves, unspeakably awful to tip when she left. But she was spared this, though the parlour-maid who appeared was pretty daunting in herself, tall and stately and grey-haired, wearing a most attractive green uniform. It was a great deal smarter than Stacy's frock; and the wearer had a cold grey eye which, Stacy was perfectly certain, noted that fact in an instant. ... No! She *would not* let herself think of that sort of thing.

"Here she is, Father!" said Agatha gladly, with a gladness that, Stacy felt, was half due to bringing home a wanted guest and half due to reaching home again after even a brief absence. And Sir Humphrey, looking absolutely as if these surroundings were only natural to him, shook hands and welcomed her, and said, Was it to be Miss Anastasia, or Miss Stacy? and was sternly bidden by Agatha to drop any sort of Miss, and laughed, and was as jolly as possible, making Stacy feel as much at home as she could possibly feel at such short notice in such palatial surroundings.

"Oh, I do hope you'll enjoy being here!" said Agatha.

"I'm quite sure I shall!" said Stacy. And so she did, though
it took a little time to get accustomed to this lap of luxury.
She wasn't used to early tea, brought by a housemaid nearly
as stately as the parlour-maid, or to having her bath turned on
next door and everything arranged there for her—in fact, the
first morning she had the wildest hunt for sponge and towels,
before she found them all in neat order beside the bath. She
wasn't used to a breakfast where the sideboard groaned under
an array of dishes hot and cold, and one just went and chose
out whatever pleased one best. She wasn't used to having a car
whenever she wanted to go out, or to meals of such splendour,
or to great magnificent grounds to wander about, or to parties
where everything happened as if by clockwork, without any
fuss beforehand, or any need for Agatha or herself to lift a
finger. It was like being transported, with her eyes wide open,
into some wonderland of dreams.

"It's so nice that you like doing *everything*!" said Agatha
happily when they had driven, and played tennis, and picnicked,
and bathed in the lovely pool that lay behind the house.

"Well, it's all so lovely!" said Stacy with all her heart.

Indeed, in far less gorgeous surroundings she would have
been perfectly happy with her adored Agatha. It is said that one
day of inhabiting the same house is a greater test of friendship
than a year of casual meetings; and, if that is the case, Agatha
stood the test well. She was just as sweet and dear as she had
seemed at school, where they had been in different boarding-
houses. She quite evidently found her greatest pleasure in
doing what pleased other people.

As for Sir Humphrey, he was the perfect host—even
realizing, as few hosts do, how necessary it is for all girls to
go away and talk confidentially in secrecy for hours and hours
about nothing in particular. He laughed at them, of course,
but so delightfully that no one could have minded. He made

Stacy feel at home by teasing her soundly: asking with the utmost seriousness about all sorts of things at College, and then bringing them up against her at unexpected moments.

"I know nothing about it," he would say to some dignified dowager at some quite serious dinner party. "You must ask Miss Wayland—she learns *everything* at her College." Or, when the very alarming chef consulted him in agitation about some kitchen contretemps: "Ask Mademoiselle Wayland, Pernier— she is sure to know!" Or, when Stacy mentioned fellow-students, Dell and Palliser and Smithkins, he would interrupt in a pained voice: "*Miss* Dell, surely, and *Miss* Palliser—or is it really co-educational, and is Smithkins a young gentleman?"

He was a delightful host, running all their parties in the most perfect manner, so that every one got a fair share of tennis and attention, and no one could possibly feel overlooked, or slighted, or put upon. Indeed, it seemed sometimes to Stacy that if there were by chance—as is likely to happen at even the nicest parties—one or two guests who were plain or dull or unpopular, by their side Sir Humphrey was unfailingly to be found—if, indeed, Agatha was not there before him.

She was exceedingly popular. So much Stacy saw immediately, with the greatest joy and no surprise at all. There was always a little knot of people wherever she went, sometimes girls— Agatha was always happy with her own sex—even more often men. Stacy, fatherless and brotherless, and accustomed only to the unattractive companionship of Mr. Phipps and his son Howard, found herself a little shy and stiff with strange menfolks, and envied (without the least jealousy) Agatha's easy unaffected manner of dealing with them. It seemed extraordinary that such a wonderfully attractive girl should not have been long ago engaged or even married—Stacy was quite sure that it could be from no lack of opportunity. She said as much to Agatha in a sudden little outburst one evening, as they lingered over good-nights in her room.

Agatha, who never talked of that sort of thing, blushed, and looked a little unhappy.

"You *must* have had proposals, Agatha!" Stacy persisted, bold now that she had broken the ice.

"Oh ... well ... yes," Agatha admitted reluctantly; and then quickly, "but don't let's talk about it, Stacy! You can't think how horrible it is to hurt people when you say 'No.'"

"But don't you ever mean to say 'Yes'?"

"Not till I've found some one whom I like as well as Father!" said Agatha. And Stacy felt, as she had felt many a time before, that it must be quite wonderful to possess a father who is so perfect as to be one's ideal.

She felt a little compassion for a visitor of that afternoon who had quite evidently been swept off his feet by the mere sight of Agatha: a tall thin young parson in very aged flannels, who had come in the train of the squire's wife from the next village. Lady Marjorie was easily the most popular person in the county, a merry chatterer who seemed always on the outlook for doing a kindness to some one.

"I simply *made* him come, *much* against his will, poor darling," she confessed gaily to Agatha in her emphatic way. "I'd asked him to luncheon to-day *purposely*. His name is Blount, and he comes from the other end of nowhere—Chapel Cloud, nine miles from anywhere! A great rambling old vicarage with mullioned windows and the most heavenly views, and not a soul to speak to—he'll turn into a hermit there in no time. Such a *pity*! But I'm sure you and your father will be good to him."

They were, of course—Agatha was perhaps too good and too charming. The young man, who had been so reluctant to come, was equally reluctant to go; he had had no eyes, for the last couple of hours, for any one but his young hostess. ... But Stacy knew well enough that it would never do to allude to that, either then or afterwards. She dreamed, when Agatha had at last said good-night and gone off to her own room, that Mr. Blount had come to their next tennis party dressed in a Fauntleroy suit with a blue sash, showing an incredible amount of long thin leg at the end of his black velvet knickers, and explaining that his only flannels had fallen to pieces—as, indeed, seemed not unlikely. Stacy was so sorry for him that she woke up, saying so out loud; and the moon was shining full on her face, and she pulled her curtains to shut it out, and fell asleep again very soundly.

There was only one thing forbidden to Agatha—she was not allowed to drive a car. ("You see what a silly Father thinks me!" she said, in her sweet smiling way, to Stacy without the least sign of grousing. And: "You see how valuable I think her!" Sir Humphrey responded.) As, however, if he himself couldn't drive her, there were always two chauffeurs at her beck and call, the hardship was not great. It was on the next day after the aforementioned tennis party that, Sir Humphrey being away for the day, the two girls set off on a foolish feminine expedition of their own.

"Not in a big car," Agatha explained, "because there are all sorts of darling roads that I've always wanted to explore, and Father always says he couldn't get through there. But we'll just go out, and turn wherever it looks interesting, and take heaps of food so that it doesn't matter if we get lost." And, since the spell of her enchantment seemed to have fallen on all servants connected with the place, the head chauffeur condescended to take them himself, in a smallish car of rather high horse-power, on this childish and undignified expedition.

The little winding roads were, certainly, most attractive: though in some places even the smallish car found a difficulty in getting through, and Agatha's fairy godmother alone knew what would have happened if they had met anything. A rule was made, and solemnly kept, that each girl should choose in turn whenever there was any choice of way. And so they went uphill and downhill, and across the most hateful little spiteful

bridges, and up and up and up to a high peaky moor where
children were picking bilberries with purple-dyed fingers;
and Agatha would have bought any quantity of these to take
home if Barkis, the head chauffeur, had not at last entered
a remonstrance, out of regard for his cushions. So Agatha,
sweet and compliant at once, gave the children sixpence all
round instead; and they drove on farther to the best view they
had seen yet—which was saying much—and drew up there
for luncheon, Barkis retiring, with a stately modesty, behind a
neighbouring hillock with his share, so that the girls might be
unembarrassed by his presence.

"How glorious it is up here!" Stacy cried, eating the most
heavenly chicken sandwiches with vast enjoyment.

"And it's such fun not knowing in the least where we are!"
Agatha agreed happily. "And isn't it marvellous, Stacy, to go all
these miles and miles and never meet a soul?"

Stacy agreed with all her heart. As a matter of fact, she
appreciated this a great deal more than Agatha, being
accustomed to a town with the most hideous amount of
traffic, where one half expected to brush small children off the
spokes of one's bicycle if one ever ventured to ride it. But as
Stacy didn't possess a bicycle, she only knew this disadvantage
by hearsay.

It would hardly be tactful (considering that neither was any
longer a schoolgirl) to say how much they managed to eat up
there in that fresh, clear air. And then they wandered about a
little, quite thrilled actually to see a couple of farm-houses and
a little church standing up on the top of the next hill, solitary
in the lonely landscape. And then Barkis came up to suggest
with all respect that the afternoon was getting on, and, as he
had no idea of the way home … Agatha agreed reluctantly
that perhaps they ought to be thinking of going back; and they
got into the car again and drove rapidly on towards the next
hill and the little church.

It was not so near as it looked. There was a sudden deep dip that took them down into an unsuspected valley, and then a tedious long stiff climb on the far side, Barkis looking grimly at the narrow rough road, with most evident thoughts of his tyres. And quite suddenly, as they neared the top, the car stopped with a little choking cough. ... Stacy, who knew nothing whatever about cars, thought that it sounded exactly like the last gasp of a faithful animal who has been overdriven.

"What is it, Barkis?" Agatha asked out of the window. But Barkis, examining, couldn't say at all. He looked very much discomfited indeed. He looked around, and up, and down; but there wasn't anything to be seen of a hopeful nature except the two farmhouses and the little church up the hill—and they hadn't seen such a thing as an A.A. man for hours.

"There might be a garage ..." said Barkis.

"We'll get out and see," said Agatha. "Come, Stacy!"

Though the hill was steep, it really was not unpleasant to walk sharply, after sitting still for so many hours. Agatha observed brightly that it was a darling little old church. Stacy was sure that there *must* be some sort of garage ... But there wasn't. At the top of the hill they looked down another steep, sharp descent, with a few scattered cottages here and there. There was a little red letter-box fixed in the wall opposite the church announcing that, unlikely as it seemed, a collection was actually made there every day; but otherwise it seemed to Stacy that they had reached the other end of nowhere. ... And, just as that mental phrase struck her with an odd familiarity, Agatha cried:

"Here's somebody coming! ... Why, it's Mr. Blount!"

Stacy had seen that at once: had seen, too, the look that he gave Agatha as she spoke. He stared and stared, with his heart in his eyes, and had no word to say.

"The car's broken down," Stacy cut in quickly—he would

be most awfully embarrassed when he realized how long and how silently he had gazed. "Is there a—a garage, or anything?"

He came to himself with a jump and a flush, speaking quickly in a queer dazed voice.

"Garage? No! I'm afraid the nearest is nine miles away."

("Nine miles from anywhere." Lady Marjorie's voice rang in Stacy's memory.)

"Is this your church?" Agatha asked in her pretty soft voice. "Chapel Cloud? What a charming name!"

He was going off into a sort of walking swoon again, gazing and gazing; it wouldn't do at all! Stacy cut in quite sharply.

"But what are we to *do*? The car is stuck, nearly at the top of the hill; and we've got to get back somehow!"

He shook himself awake again, and became suddenly business-like and most urgently anxious to be of use. He knew a certain amount about cars himself—he would go and see what he could do. In the meantime would they—would they go in and have some tea or something? Yes, that was the Rectory—an enormous place. He let it to parishioners, who farmed the land; and he just lived with them.

It was indeed an enormous place, with at least twelve bedroom windows staring blankly down at them; and his study, into which he agitatedly conducted the girls, was huge and high and bare, and extraordinarily comfortless. His books seemed lost in plain rough wooden shelves. There was no desk, only an immense plain wooden table. There were several plain hard chairs, and two very aged wickerwork ones with torn cushions—of which he was most unhappily aware as he inducted Agatha and Stacy into them. Hurriedly murmuring that Mrs. Price would bring them tea, he fled; and Stacy, looking round with a severe domestically scientific eye, noted all the deficiencies of the place—and there were a great many of them. The unknown Mrs. Price seemed no great hand with

Would they go in and have some tea?

either broom or duster or needle—there had been a great hole in the back of his sock, showing above his shoe, and the cushions were almost past mending from neglect …

"What a wonderful view!" Agatha murmured. And so there was, through most beautiful stone mullioned windows. After all, there are other points of view besides that of Domestic Science.

The unknown Mrs. Price pushed open the door, and banged in with a kitchen tray containing tea things. She was extremely Welsh, with a soft sing-song voice, and black hair, and little quick black eyes like currants. Now some Welsh women are the best servants and housekeepers in the world, and some are—at the other extreme. Mrs. Price belonged to the second class. She pattered out a long string of questions and comments, staring hard; she dumped the tray down on the wooden table near Stacy; she banged out again, staring back to the last over the shoulder of her torn cotton dress.

"*This* tea wasn't made with boiling water!" said Stacy with strong distaste. "Mind the chipped spout, Agatha; it's slopping all over the place. Give me the hot water and I'll rinse out the cups *before* we drink out of them. … Heavens, she's cut the butter with an oniony knife!"

They stared at each other and burst out laughing. It was the only possible way to bear it. But:

"Oh, *poor* Mr. Blount!" said Agatha compassionately.

"Yes, indeed!" Stacy agreed. "Thank goodness, here's a dog! Do you think he'll drink sour milk?"

He did, with pleasure; and snapped up chunks of onionish bread and butter without winking. ("He's evidently used to it," said Stacy.) And so, when presently Mr. Blount returned with the heartening news that he and Barkis had found and righted whatever was wrong, he was cheered by the sight of empty plates and cups that had evidently been used—for his first glance was consciously anxious. The black-and-white Cocker spaniel, beating a welcoming tail hard on the dusty floor, told no tales; and the weedy bed of discouraged flowers, just outside the window, was wet from a recent shower, and did not betray that its latest wetting came from the teapot.

"I hope Mrs. Price looked after you all right?" said Mr. Blount a little doubtfully and faintly; and Agatha and Stacy, carefully looking in different directions, murmured polite nothings—hurriedly going on to admire the view, about which it was easy enough to be enthusiastic: though if the windows had been cleaned within the last six months or so it would have made an even better show.

And so they went down to the waiting Barkis, very anxious to be off again; and they repeated their thanks, and got into the car, and slid rapidly away down the steep hill. And Mr. Blount, looking after them a very long time when they were quite lost to sight, went back into his dusty study and sat down in the chair which had held Agatha; and the Cocker spaniel put a damp black nose on his knee to comfort him.

CHAPTER V

The Second Holidays

NATURALLY, no one was at the station to meet Stacy; she had never expected it. Trains are late, and stations are crowded, on the twenty-third of December; and, in any case, she was not due in until after the children's bedtime—even if Aunt Monica had liked waiting about in a crowded station for a late train. As for Mr. Phipps *(never* Uncle Paul), it would not be at all in his line to waste valuable time in performing a kindness which would bring him no return. So Stacy lugged her own heavy suitcase down the platform, and vainly hailed quite a lot of taxis before one condescended to see her signal and respond to it. There were a great many people about that night who looked much better able to tip worthily than the shabby schoolgirlish person with the very shabby luggage. ... It would, of course, be reckoned against her that she had gone to this extravagance at all, instead of walking and having her case sent by an out-porter; but she was extremely tired, and the night was wet and raw, and she simply could not walk up that long hill with the sleet driving in her face.

She heard of her waste of money, of course, even sooner than she expected, for it was Howard who opened the door to her—Howard, who should have been in bed half an hour before.

"Did you come in a *taxi*, Anastasia?" was his greeting in shrill shocked accents.

"Yes, I did. And please let me come in at once, out of the rain," said Stacy. If she spoke rather sharply it may perhaps be forgiven her.

The taxi-man lumbered up the steps with her suit-case,

grunting to show how heavy it was, accepted her money in far from a Christmas spirit, though she had paid nearly double his legal fare, clumped heavily down again in a vengeful silence. Howard, meanwhile, was preceding her down the passage, proclaiming her arrival and her crime in no uncertain tones.

"Here's Anastasia! And she came in a *taxi*!"

"Anastasia! I hope you are not ill?" Mrs. Phipps cried alarmedly.

"Not at all, thank you, Aunt Monica. Only very tired."

"What a relief!" said Mrs. Phipps, referring, obviously, to the first sentence, and quite uninterested in the second.

"It would have been pretty dreadful if she had been ill, wouldn't it," Howard contributed shrilly, "seeing that we haven't got any servant!"

Stacy's heart, none too light to start with, dropped like a stone. She had been thanking her stars, over and over again during that weary journey, that at least her late arrival would have freed her from the eternal stoning of raisins. But there are worse kitchen jobs than that, as she knew well enough by this time.

"Has Theodosia left, then?" she inquired blankly.

"Didn't I tell you?" Mrs. Phipps returned in rather an embarrassed tone, looking anywhere except at the returned wanderer. "Oh, yes! Most tiresome! She wanted to go home for some family wedding on Boxing Day; there was a … a little uncomfortableness about it, and she said at last that she didn't want to come back."

"And you haven't found any one else?"

"So difficult, just at this time of year!" Mrs. Phipps murmured hastily. "And—but you must be very tired, Anastasia! I am sure you would like to go up to your room now, and we can talk about things after supper."

Stacy left the room in perfect silence, lugging her suit-case up the steep stairs without a word. There was no need for talk about "things." She had come back from a year at her College—nearly at the end of her course, naturally well able to turn her hand to almost anything about a household. It would save a whole month's wages to do without any servant until she was due to return again. ... Her bed wasn't made, the room was undusted, there was no water in the jug ... She fiercely fought back the lump that rose in her throat. It was all perfectly hateful, of course; but her holidays (so-called) had always been hateful here—and this, thank goodness, was the very last of them!

Though the room was stone-cold, she took her time about going down again; and while she was unpacking the fire kindled—speaking, of course, in a strictly metaphorical manner. She was a year older than when she had last left that unattractive little room; she had learned a great deal in a great many ways, she was no longer a schoolgirl—she had, in fact, grown up.

If Mr. and Mrs. Phipps had not realized that, it was time they did. ... And, in any case, she was to be free of them for ever at the end of this coming term.

"What a long time you have been, Anastasia!" Mrs. Phipps commented nervously on her reappearance. "I was hoping that you would have helped me with the supper. ..."

"I had to get my room ready, Aunt Monica," said Stacy without apology.

"Oh—oh, I am afraid you had! I am so sorry. ... Howard, will you tell your father that supper is ready?"

"So Howard sits up to supper now?" Stacy commented amicably.

"Well, he has been helping me a good deal, since Theodosia left. And, of course, he is getting a big boy now," said Mrs. Phipps.

"Yes," said Stacy. "Of course, we are all a good deal older since I was here last. ... How do you do, Mr. Phipps?"

She rose and shook hands politely, and their eyes met with a little shock of dislike on both sides. Her remark had been double-edged, with intention; and he recognized this if Mrs. Phipps did not. Also, she had never before definitely addressed him like that by his name; she had only avoided saying Uncle Paul.

It was an uncomfortable supper; and that not merely because the food was badly cooked and badly served—as Stacy, after a year of learning the best way to do everything, recognized very disagreeably. Mrs. Phipps was in one of her most die-away moods: almost too tired to eat or speak, and quietly determined that every one should know it. Howard was very anxious to retail the important part which he had played in the household: "I did do the potatoes well, didn't I, Mother?" "You would have been much more tired if I hadn't helped you!" "*I* beat the eggs, Anastasia!" "Father, do *you* know the proper way to separate the white from the yolk?" Mr. Phipps ate with a rather puckered mouth, and said little. Only, as he rose from the table, he remarked pointedly that his wife must lie on the drawing-room sofa for the rest of the evening and not over-exert herself any more. "*You* will see to the washing-up, I am sure, Anastasia?"

"Certainly," said Stacy, still most politely.

She was reserving her forces for the battle that was to come. This evening was an unsuitable time for it.

She lay in bed next morning of set purpose: not because she was asleep, for that was frankly impossible. The shrill voice of Howard pervaded the house: upstairs, downstairs, at the front door, at the back door, even out on the steps. ("I am doing these steps very nicely, don't you think, Mother? Theodosia *never* got them so clean!") Mrs. Phipps was also heard, responding dolorously. Even the whining tones of Mona reached finally to Stacy's pillow, complaining that she couldn't fasten something without assistance. And, at that point, it seemed time to get up.

Stacy came down, to find the family just seating itself at breakfast; and she sat down too, with polite but chilly greetings exchanged all round. Mrs. Phipps was already drooping in her chair, though there didn't seem much occasion for it, as nothing had been cooked but boiled eggs and tea. Mr. Phipps had never looked more black, more bleak, more unattractively like Mr. Murdstone. He ate in perfect silence. Then he rolled up his table-napkin with extreme neatness, and spoke.

"Your aunt is extremely tired, Anastasia."

"Yes. She must be, with no servant," Stacy agreed blandly.

"I am surprised that you did not come down in time to help her."

"I was very tired too," Stacy replied unmoved. "We work very hard at College, and it is a long term; and I did not get here, you know, until after eight last night."

Mr. Phipps bent his head stiffly in acknowledgment of this excuse—which Stacy had not meant for an excuse.

"That is, of course, true. But I am sure that, having had a good *long* night's rest, you will do all you can to help her."

Stacy did not answer this at all, so that, after a short and blank pause, Mr. Phipps was obliged to look directly at her. The brown eyes and the black met with another little shock of dislike.

"You have not answered me, Anastasia."

"No," said Stacy. "I was wondering how to put it, so that you would really understand. ... You see, as I've said before, I have finished a very hard term, and I am going back to the hardest of all, and the most important. I don't get a very long holiday. I think it ought to *be* a holiday. If I go back tired out, I shan't do well in my final exam; and that matters a great deal. If I do badly in it, I shan't get a good job afterwards."

Mr. Phipps was a good man of business. He considered this statement attentively before he answered it.

"I understand all that, Anastasia. But I should hardly suppose that doing a little housework, to help your aunt, would overtire a naturally strong girl."

Stacy's temper rose.

"Even when you had Theodosia, Mr. Phipps, I think I've always helped a good deal in the house!"

Mr. Phipps raised sceptical eyebrows; and Stacy controlled herself quickly. She must keep herself thoroughly well in hand if she wished to win this all-important battle.

"What I mean is this. Of course, I am willing to help—I

Stacy's temper rose.

always have been. But do you expect me to take the place of a servant, now that you haven't got one?"

"You are being a little hysterical, I think," Mr. Phipps reproved her coldly. "The position is unfortunate, I own, just at Christmas time; but we are all willing to help, to endure perhaps a little discomfort, for a short time. …"

"*How* short a time?" Stacy shot at him.

"Really, Anastasia, you are being childish!" Mrs. Phipps broke in weakly. "You *know* how difficult it is to get a new servant, especially in the winter."

"Are you trying to get one?" Stacy shot back at her. "Or are you meaning to carry on—until I go back to College?"

Her point was well scored; her arrow had gone home in more than one direction. Mrs. Phipps coloured an uncomfortable, unbecoming pink. Howard stared eagerly from father to mother, as if he knew all about it, which was probably the case. Mr. Phipps looked at Stacy with an acid dislike.

"This is all very disagreeable …"

"Very!" Stacy agreed instantly.

"… and there is no need to continue the discussion. I wish to know whether you are prepared to make yourself useful—or not."

Stacy drew a deep breath. Fortunately her wits were quick. She had expected this very question, and was ready for it.

"What you really mean, of course, is—am I prepared to do the work that Theodosia has always done, as well as the work that Aunt Monica has always expected of me?"

She waited for a reply which did not come. Mr. Phipps only continued to look at her distastefully.

"Very well, then—yes, I am! But only until you can find a proper servant. I must have at least the last fortnight of my holiday for a real rest."

The brow of Mr. Phipps relaxed. He had obviously not

expected such a ready surrender. "That will be quite satisfactory, then ..."

"Wait!" said Stacy, with her head up and her eyes very bright. "If I do this, I shall of course expect to be paid the same wages as you paid Theodosia, and to have the same outings— half of every Sunday entirely to myself, and one long half-day once a week. She had a free day a month, too, I know; but, as I don't propose to take her place for a month, I won't say anything about that."

The weak mouth of Mrs. Phipps had dropped open in consternation, and she stared forlornly at her husband. Only she knew how much of the household work had been dropped on Stacy's shoulders during those half-Sundays and weekly holidays.

"Really, Anastasia," said Mr. Phipps acidly, "I am surprised that you should haggle like this! Between relations, or connections, it is surely quite unseemly to debate a mere matter of a pound or two."

Stacy's brown eyes, growing brighter and brighter, were turned full upon him.

"But you explained to me, last time I was here, that all you had done for me was upon a business basis! You made me understand that most particularly—and I am only trying to be business-like now. ... And, by the way, as I was not here either at Easter or in the summer to be an expense to you, there surely must be a little money due to me, which I should be very glad to have."

She had got him fairly upon the raw now. He stood up with a sharp movement, which upset his teacup.

"I am astonished at you, Anastasia! This discussion is most unseemly ..."

"Father, you've upset your tea on the *clean* cloth!" Howard piped up officiously; while Mona, for once in accord with her brother, chimed in: "All *methy*!"

Mr. Phipps slammed the door upon a muttered last word—but not soon enough.

"Mother," Howard cried virtuously, "did you hear what Father said? He said—"

"Come along, Howard, and help me clear and wash up," said Stacy hastily—she could well afford to be magnanimous now. "Just tell me what you want to have cooked for luncheon, Aunt Monica, and I'll see to it all while you rest. ... Besides, you will be wanting to go to the Registry Office early, won't you? I expect they will close this afternoon."

Now that her battle was fought and won, she was willing enough to show her household skill. Aunt Monica *did* look tired out. The kitchen was likely to be a howling wilderness. There was all the interminable Christmas cookery to attack. ...

"But I'm getting my wages, and my two half-days a week—half Boxing Day, too, of course!" said Stacy to herself, with her chin in the air. "And, thank goodness, this is the last Christmas that I'll ever, ever spend here!"

CHAPTER VI

The Int.

STACY'S words came true. Her triumph was complete. She had a very hectic Christmas, of course. Between them, the departing Theodosia and the feckless Aunt Monica had reduced the kitchen to a state which might have made angels weep—supposing those bright beings to have any acquaintance with Domestic Science. But the Christmas cookery was a sheer triumph from start to finish; and Stacy sallied forth, a free woman, on Boxing Day, and went to a matinée, and ate luxuriously at a tea-shop in peace and comfort, and went straight to her bed when she came in, being pretty tired—yes, heartlessly deaf to cross wails from Mona, who was apt to be upset after rich food, and the moaning sound of Aunt Monica's voice as she wrestled with her; and shutting an offended nose to certain unsavoury kitchen smells which cried aloud that Howard was wrestling unsuccessfully with the supper. And she took her (or Theodosia's) half-day on Thursday, and enjoyed herself thoroughly; and on the following Sunday she went out on the stroke of two—and by that time Mrs. Phipps found it well to engage in haste (subsequently repenting at leisure) a successor to Theodosia, who rejoiced in the name of Doris-Elaine-Rosina.

Mr. Phipps grimly paid up the ten days' wages that had been earned, and even added a small sum on account of the Easter and Summer holidays that had been spent elsewhere; and Stacy returned to her College like a giant refreshed. Was there ever a red-haired person who did not enjoy a fight for the sheer love of it?

It was rather hateful, of course, that this should be her

last term in a place where she had been extremely happy and had made hosts of friends; but rather thrilling, too, to think of earning her own living, being her own mistress, making still more new friends in some pleasant unknown sphere. Old students were constantly dashing back for a night, or even only a few hours, eager to hear College news and impart their own adventures, which were invariably either foul or marvellous. Some were engaged, or even married. Some were earning fabulous salaries, and mightily enjoying themselves at the same time. Stacy, who had never been a slacker, worked harder than ever, that she might do well in her final exam and join the throng of these independent and successful people.

There came a day when Miss Pim, the Principal, sent for her; tiny Miss Pim, five foot nothing, with a voice almost impossibly soft and gentle, before whose lightest word the whole College trembled. She had had an application for a cook from a large girls' school in Dorset: a hundred and thirty girls; salary seventy-five pounds a year. Stacy had better apply for the post.

Stacy, appalled, murmured that she had never thought of beginning with a single-handed job of such magnitude. She had expected to begin as an underling and work up. Did the Principal really think that she could do it?

"If I did not think so, I should not have recommended you for the post," said Miss Pim in her voice of silk. And that, of course, being quite final, Stacy duly made her application, and was bidden to come and be interviewed; and dressed herself in her best—which wasn't anything to boast of—and travelled down to Dorset with her heart in her new brown shoes.

It was pretty terrible; not in the least like dear St. Alkmund's. The buildings were so fine, and the grounds so enormous, and it was so obviously a school for the daughters of the very rich. But the headmistress was kind and encouraging (which cheeringly meant, of course, that Miss Pim's recommendation had been very good indeed) and seemed to take kindly to the trembling Stacy. And she was actually engaged at that stupendous salary; and she stayed the night in a delightful guest-room, and found a large bowl of fruit awaiting her pleasure there, and was given early tea in the morning. Supper, of course, had been a terrific ordeal, with so many strange eyes upon her. But every one had been kind and encouraging, and the outgoing cook (who was leaving to be married) gave a cheering account of her many duties; and Stacy returned to College on the crest of the wave. It all seemed too good to be true! The only drawback to the post—the very short holidays—was in her eyes rather a recommendation, since she would have no home to go to.

She went up to Miss Pim's office again, this time trembling not at all, and reported her good news, and was very kindly congratulated. Short holidays? No, she did not mind that in the least! Had she found the headmistress pleasant? Yes, *very*!

"Yes, you would. I expected that," said Miss Pim. "I may as well tell you, now that you've got the post, that that will perhaps sometimes be a difficulty. She is too kind. She can't bear to say 'No' to anybody."

Stacy looked a little puzzled, and a very little alarmed.

"Nothing to be afraid of!" said Miss Pim, seeing this, as she saw everything. "She is a charming person; I've known her for years. In fact, this is by far the best post of this term; and I'm glad to give it to my best student."

Stacy, scarlet to the roots of her red hair, could hardly believe her ears. But there was actually a kindly twinkle in the small, keen blue eyes that could, on occasion, look like chilled steel.

"That will do, Miss Wayland," said Miss Pim immediately afterwards in quite her usual manner. "Please send Miss Smithkins to me."

Which Stacy did; soon after meeting that young lady,

anything but pleased with either her lot or her Principal. She had spent her year at College working a very little and playing a great deal; and she had just applied for a post and failed to get it.

"You were in luck to have a good int., Wayland! Mine was perfectly *foul.*"

Yes, Stacy agreed with all her heart, she *had* been lucky, extraordinarily lucky. She went and wrote a stiff little note to Mrs. Phipps, announcing her success; and in due course received a stiff little answer of congratulation. Possibly Aunt Monica was quite as much relieved at her state of independence as she could be herself.

The rest of the term flew like lightning. The dreadful final exam came and went; and sometimes Stacy hoped that she had done well in it, and sometimes she feared that she had come the most fearful cropper—which would be simply terrible, letting down Miss Pim and the College even more than herself. It was a relief that she would not know the result for weeks and weeks—not until she had safely dug herself into her Dorset school, and shown her mettle there.

It was at that point that Fate, hitherto so kind, suddenly showed the other side of her Janus-face. Stacy, flying up to her room to enjoy a letter from Agatha, stood in dismay by the window, reading and re-reading.

> "DARLING STACY,—I *am* so disappointed not to
> have you these next holidays as we had planned;
> but the spring has been so cold that Father says he
> simply can't face England at present …"

And so on: all quite genuine, all quite reasonable, but a dreadful blow in the face for Stacy, with nowhere else to go. Agatha knew by this time what sort of holidays all those school ones had been, and why Stacy had infinitely preferred term time. She had insistently begged her to spend the Easter holidays with them, wherever they might be, and had refused to take any refusal. But that had been, of course, on the supposition that Sir Humphrey would have found an English home, and more or less settled down in it, by the beginning of April. It wasn't a practical proposition when he and Agatha were still wandering round the isles of Greece for the next month or so.

"*Please* don't worry. I *quite* understand," Stacy wrote back at once to Agatha, who was obviously dreadfully distressed over her defalcation. "It will be all right—and, anyhow, I should only have had about a week or ten days." She went on to tell (in very different terms from those of her letter to Mrs. Phipps) all about the Dorset school, and how terrifying the prospect of her int. had been, and how delightful the headmistress had proved; and about the tennis courts, and the swimming pool, and the great gymnasium; and how, though really the cook, she would rank as Staff, and have the most tremendous fun with all those young mistresses, who had been perfectly topping to her. It would be hard and responsible work, of course, but she didn't mind that. And she didn't mind, as many people would have done, the shortness of her holidays, because in her position that was rather a boon than otherwise. ... In any case, Agatha was definitely *not* to feel guilty or anxious about Easter.

But for all these brave words, it was in reality a terrible blow. Stacy would only have a couple of pounds in hand at the end of the term; and she couldn't, *wouldn't*, cadge for hospitality from the Phippses. ... Perhaps she might find some sort of temporary job; what it was would matter nothing, if only it afforded her board and lodging. She summoned up all her courage and went with her difficulty to the Principal, who was kind, but not hopeful. Jobs for a week or ten days were not easy to find. "And besides, Miss Wayland, you ought to get a *holiday*, in justice to yourself as well as to your new post."

Yes! Stacy knew that, and owned it; and retired from the Presence in a sadly chastened frame of mind. That obstinately empty ten days swelled to gigantic proportions … and then suddenly dwindled all to nothing, like a pricked balloon, compared with the much greater blow that fell upon her.

Her correspondence was not a large one, consisting only of letters from a few St. Alkmund's girls. It was easy to pick out at sight, from among these, the stiff, expensive envelope with the Dorset postmark; and Stacy tore it open excitedly. It was just possible—and how beautifully that would solve all her difficulties!—that the headmistress would like her to go straight to the school at the end of College term, getting, of course, the holiday that she needed, but at the same time learning her way about the place, so that she might start fair. It would save a lot of time. It would be most convenient. It would …

Stacy stood staring at her open letter, and her face had turned quite white. It was so kind, so apologetic; even (if such a thing can be said of a headmistress) just a little shamefaced. Miss Wayland would understand and forgive. The circumstances were *so* unusual. She would see that it had been impossible to add to Miss Tomlinson's trouble. …

In short, Miss Tomlinson, the present cook, had broken her engagement—or had had it broken for her—and had begged to stay on.

"Miss Pim wants you, Wayland."

With her letter in her pocket Stacy staggered blindly upstairs to the office, and found her Principal with another letter, of similar appearance, in her hand and the alarming look of chilled steel in her eyes.

"You have heard, too, Miss Wayland? I am extremely sorry—more sorry than I can say. I did warn you, I think, that Miss Pontifex is one of those people who can never bear to say 'No.'"

"It's all right. It can't be helped," Stacy stammered out. "It would have been frightfully rough luck on Miss Tomlinson, when she's in trouble, to have to get out."

Not the language that one was accustomed to use to one's Principal! But Miss Pim, who spoke beautiful English and was apt to be scathing about what she received in return, passed poor Stacy's comment without a word, and even repeated a little of it.

"It is rough luck for you too, I am afraid."

"It can't be helped," Stacy repeated; and then looked up

Her face had turned quite white.

with a faint dawn of hope in her white face. "You don't know of anything else? It wouldn't be so good, of course; I don't expect that. But *anything* …"

Miss Pim, shaking her head, looked quite genuinely distressed.

"I am more sorry than I can tell you to say 'No,' Miss Wayland. But I had rather unusually few applications this term; and I have already filled every vacant post that I know of."

"It can't be helped," said Stacy for the third time, very faintly; and went down to the Reading Room to scan frantically the pages of Situations Vacant in one paper after another. … She had felt so superior, only the day before, when she saw Smithkins and a few other unplaced students doing the very same thing, with long faces and drooping heads. … And only ten days of the term remained.

Nine days of term left, and no ray of hope. Eight days, and every paper still blandly useless.

Seven days …

Stacy sat staring at something that might just possibly be of use to her.

> "Two elderly gentlewomen require, as soon as possible, a LADY COOK, College-trained preferred. Excellent references essential. Comfortable home. Own room. State salary and experience. Apply Box 725."

Stacy was not the girl to let the grass grow under her feet. The next post, at the corner pillar-box, was collected in twenty minutes; and it contained a letter addressed to Box 725. Nothing might come of it, of course; but, on the other hand, it might—and there was nothing else in any paper of the slightest likelihood.

By return of post—and now there were only five days

left—came an answer. Miss W. Postgate presented her compliments, in a pointed old-fashioned writing, to Miss Wayland, and would be glad to see her, between the hours of three and five, at 17 St. Philibert's Terrace, Upper Galting, S.W.10. Stacy, taking this in fear and trembling to Miss Pim— for she was so incredibly particular as to where she planted out her students—received an unexpectedly lenient reply.

"By an odd chance, I happen to know the Vicar of St. Philibert's, Upper Galting. If he knows these people, you may go for an interview, Miss Wayland. ... Trunk call, please, Miss Tracy. ... Wait a few minutes, Miss Wayland."

Stacy, waiting with her heart in her mouth, listened presently to that most maddeningly tantalizing thing, a one-sided telephone conversation, for no one ever had a more strictly poker-face than the Principal, and it was impossible to tell whether or no she was satisfied with her information. It seemed a very long time before she said, "Thank you very much!" and hung up the receiver.

"It seems to be quite satisfactory, Miss Wayland; but, of course, I could find out no details of any sort."

"Oh, no, Miss Pim!"

"You should go to-day, naturally."

"Oh, *yes*, Miss Pim!"

The Principal looked critically at Stacy's eager and excited face.

"Don't be too sure that anything will come of it. ... You want this post very much?"

"I *must* find something before the end of the term."

"Well," said Miss Pim, rather slowly, "don't be too enthusiastic; and don't promise things that you will find it impossible to perform. And, mind! You are *not* to accept less than thirty pounds a year."

Stacy said nothing to that—she would almost have gone for nothing, to earn her board and lodging—and a very slow smile dawned on Miss Pim's face as she continued to watch her.

"Don't forget, besides, that I expect my students to *stay* in their first posts long enough to secure a really solid recommendation when they move on."

"Oh, *yes*, Miss Pim!" said Stacy. (Didn't every one know that? Wasn't it well drilled into them from the very beginning of their training? Two years, if possible. No leaving for frivolous reasons. No accepting a post, therefore, without making sure that it was likely to be a satisfactory proposition all round.)

"Very well, then. Come and tell me the result as soon as you come back."

"Oh, *yes*, Miss Pim!"

Smithkins and her friends, hearing that they could have the advertisements to themselves in future, were first inquisitive, and then scornful.

"Well, it sounds pretty foul to me!"

"I'd rather have no job at all. What sort of screw do you expect to get?"

"*I* wouldn't be seen dead in a suburb!"

"Wouldn't you?" said Stacy, and went away, a little dashed but still considerably thrilled, to change into her best clothes that were so undeniably shabby.

"What an ass Wayland is!" said Smithkins to her gang. "She might just as well have said *London*, when we asked where she was going, and saved her face."

Which, without the slightest doubt, she herself would infallibly have done in a similar situation.

CHAPTER VII

NUMBER SEVENTEEN

IT was a very different int. from Stacy's first. She had to cross London to a terminus that she did not know, most bewildering in its nature: dozens of platforms, hundreds of signposts, thousands of people hurrying in all directions—or, if these numbers were not exactly accurate, that was how they struck Stacy. In any case, all of them—platforms, posts, and people—looked dingy and grimy and depressing. The suburban train was all three, in a superlative degree; you couldn't touch anything that didn't come off on you.

As she had never been that way before, she had to stare out anxiously at each successive station, fearful of passing the one for which she was bound; and each seemed to her, if possible, less attractive than the one that had preceded it. But at long last the right name loomed up at her from among a setting of advertisements, and she induced the door to open most reluctantly, and looked disgustedly at its result on her glove, and jumped down on to a dirty platform, and made her way with a most uninspiring crowd of fellow-passengers to a door at the top of a flight of filthy steps. By that time her heart was so much in her shoes that she could almost have found herself hoping that she wouldn't get the job—but not quite. Anything in the world would be better than writing to Aunt Monica to say that she hadn't found anything to do.

Outside the station things were better: quite wide streets, quite decent shops. Stacy drew a breath of relief, inquired the whereabouts of St. Philibert's Terrace, found that it was within easy walking distance, and set off briskly to find it. As she went she looked about her, and made up her mind with the

utmost firmness that she wouldn't, on any account, let herself
think of the school in Dorset. That was in a perfectly remote
past; and now she wasn't *going* to get gorgeous seaside air, and
splendid bathing, and jolly young schoolmistresses to consort
with, and a great, spacious, magnificent kitchen to work in.
She had better forget all about that as fast as possible; and if
she secured this most necessary job, she must begin at once
to make notes of all the pleasant things about it. Certainly
she wouldn't have to work so hard; for the responsibility
of the Dorset school would have taxed her powers in every
direction to their utmost limit. She wouldn't be so far away
from wherever Agatha happened to settle down—-or, at
least, the chances were that that would be the case. It would
be fun to shop in London on her off-days, and to see all
sorts of interesting places that were now simply names to
her. . . .

"St. Philibert's Terrace," said a wall-sign above her head;
and Stacy took a gasping breath, like a swimmer who finds the
water pretty cold, and stood staring down it before she turned
the corner.

Well, it might have been worse—if, undeniably, it might
have been better. The road was wide, and seemed quiet;
though the prim, narrow, old-fashioned high houses were
as dismally alike as peas in a pod. Each of them had a steep
flight of steps that ran straight up off the pavement without
any vestige of garden. Each of them had prim white curtains
and short blinds, jealously guarding any secrets of their lives
from all curious passers-by. Just for a moment Stacy had a
despairing vision of a stately, spacious building set in ample
grounds that were full of trees. The next, she shook herself
mentally and physically, and identified Number Seventeen, and
ran up the steps and rang the bell without giving herself time
to think twice. If she hadn't been very quick about it there was
just a possibility that she might have turned tail and run away

altogether, as one so longs to do after ringing the dentist's
brightly polished bell.

The bell of Number Seventeen was not brightly polished,
and the handle was even less so. Stacy, regarding first one and
then the other with distaste, was suddenly aware of a very
slight movement of the closely drawn white curtain at her
immediate right. Some one was cautiously looking at her from
that vantage-ground—and it didn't seem fair. She caught just
a glimpse of a round pale-blue eye, and a bit of round pale-
pink cheek, and a wisp of pale-yellow hair above. Then the

Some one was cautiously looking at her.

curtain was quickly dropped, as if the peeper were desperately afraid of being caught at it, and at the same moment the door opened.

"Miss Postgate?" Stacy inquired politely, wishing that her voice didn't shake so. She had to look quite a long way down at the very small lady standing before her.

"I am Miss Postgate. Is this Miss Wayland? Please come in."

Stacy obeyed; and now her heart, which had been in her shoes, was in her mouth. The very narrow little hall was stuffy, in a cabbagy manner; dingy, too, with varnished yellowish paper of no particular pattern, and an old-fashioned hat-rack holding two black mackintoshes, and a drain-pipe umbrella-stand holding two black umbrellas. On the left were rather steep stairs. On the right were two doors. Behind one of these, presumably, lurked the peeper with the pale-blue eyes; but it was the second door that was opened. Stacy found herself sitting in a smallish, stiff dining-room with old-fashioned mahogany furniture considerably too large for it. The very little lady sat opposite, with her back to the light, and her eyes fixed immovably on Stacy's agitated face.

"You look very young, Miss Wayland."

"I am nineteen," Stacy told her quickly.

"You look less. What experience have you?"

"None at all. I have not yet left my Domestic Science College."

There was a brief pause, and Stacy's heart went pit-a-pat, and her brain behaved in the most extraordinary manner. How dreadful if they wouldn't have her because she was so young and so ignorant! But oh, how dreadful to come and live here! Oh, but she *must* get a job! Only five days more left. ...

Miss Postgate broke the pause by saying that perhaps the best way would be for her to describe the situation; and proceeded to do so in a stiff, deliberate manner. They had never before had a College-trained cook, but they thought

of doing so because of all the difficulties they had had with
the ordinary kind. She did not consider that the work would
be hard; they lived very simply, and the house was not large.
There was no other resident servant ("Thank goodness!"
thought Stacy, whose great dread had been that she might have
to consort at close quarters with some one quite impossible),
but a woman came in to do rough work twice a week, and a
daily maid came to do housework. She did not wish to live in,
because she was a married woman with a young child.

"You would find it dull to have all your meals alone?"

"Yes," said Stacy. "But—but I shouldn't mind that."
(Secretly, she felt herself lucky; she would have minded very
much more having to eat with the mother of the young child.)

"My sister and I are very particular about punctuality; and
we *must* have some one who will be economical and careful."

"Yes, of course!" Stacy promised readily.

"You would have the usual outings: a weekly half-day, and
half Sunday."

Stacy said "Yes" again; and felt that she was about to
become a genuine Theodosia, not merely the understudy that
she had so often been.

"About—salary," said Miss Postgate, whose hesitation
seemed to indicate that she had meant to use another word
and had changed her mind after looking again at Stacy.

"Yes?"

"It is—a little difficult. You are, of course, College trained;
but my sister and I are far from rich, and you are—very young."

"Yes," said Stacy again, trying to keep all feeling out of her
voice, but without much success.

"We are prepared to offer," said Miss Postgate slowly and
unwillingly, "thirty pounds."

Well, it wasn't much of an offer for a College student;
and Stacy had hoped for more; and Miss Pim had said that
she mustn't take less. It would be a tight fit, with clothes and

holidays … oh, but she probably wouldn't get much in the way of holidays!

"Are you satisfied with that?" said Miss Postgate, watching narrowly with her rather pale eyes, which had struck Stacy at first sight as being like those of Miss Pim.

Stacy drew a long breath, took her courage in both hands, and said, "Yes, thank you—to *begin* with."

Miss Postgate took no notice of that addition. She said, in rather a hurried voice, "By the way, I had forgotten. … I conclude you are willing to wear caps and aprons? My sister and I couldn't *dream* of anything else!"

"Oh, yes, certainly," said Stacy, who had worn uniform as a matter of course in College, and thought nothing of it either way.

Miss Postgate hesitated again, and spoke in a little, tight-lipped voice.

"And you must remember, please, that we do not allow visitors in the kitchen—at any time."

Stacy looked at her a little blankly. If she made any friends—it was just humanly possible, even in a place like Upper Galting—what *was* she to do with them, then?

"I do not expect," said Miss Postgate, tighter-lipped than ever, "to go into my kitchen at any time and find a stranger there. If, however, you have a—a sister, or any one of that sort, who may possibly wish to visit you, I am prepared to allow her to take tea with you *occasionally*. But I must always be informed beforehand."

"I see," said Stacy.

Apparently something in her tone was displeasing to Miss Postgate, for she added, in a tone that had become poker-stiff: "*Men* visitors, of course, I do not allow at *any* time! That must be clearly understood."

Stacy said obediently, "Of course," but her treacherous voice suddenly betrayed her. She hadn't any men friends to speak of, but she had a sudden sinful vision of being caught entertaining Mr. Phipps … or …

Since a certain measure of impishness goes naturally with red hair, she forgot the seriousness of this all-important interview and spoke in a voice that was as mild as milk.

"I'm not likely to have any visitors of that sort, but there is just one whom I should hate not to be allowed to ask in—if he came. He isn't likely to."

"Are you—engaged to be married?" Miss Postgate inquired, still in her poker-mood. Her tone said most effectively that, if that were the case, she didn't approve at all.

"Oh, *no*—" Stacy hastened to reassure her.

"Then, who …?"

Miss Postgate made a pause of marked displeasure.

"Only—only Sir Humphrey Phayre," Stacy murmured in her meekest possible voice.

"*Who?*"

Stacy repeated herself gently, looking down, for safety's sake, in the modestest possible manner.

"You do not mean—the *famous* Sir Humphrey Phayre?"

"Yes," Stacy meekly murmured. "His daughter Agatha is my greatest friend; we were at school together, and they have been very kind to me. If he did come—it isn't likely—I should hate to have to send him away without letting him in at all."

There was a pause. Stacy dared not, for her life, look up and show her eyes, but she had a general feeling that the pokerishness was a thing of the past.

"In such a case as that," said Miss Postgate quite agreeably, "I have no doubt that something could be arranged. … Now, will you come and see my sister?"

Presumably, then, Stacy was engaged; and for the life of her she could not have said whether she was glad or sorry. She followed the little stiff figure of her future mistress out of that room and into the one in front; and there, turning with a guilty start from the window-curtains, was another figure that was neither small, nor stiff, nor alarming.

"My sister Georgiana," said Miss Postgate. "Georgie, this is Miss Wayland of whom you have heard."

"Oh! How do you do?" said the second Miss Postgate, and half-held out her hand, in a vague manner, and then let it drop by her side, glancing dubiously at her sister. She was a large shapeless creature who looked curiously young and yet obviously wasn't. She had large pale-blue eyes like a baby's, but her pink-and-white skin was very wrinkled. Her fluffy hair looked pale yellow, until one looked closer and discovered that it was greyish and thin.

"Miss Wayland, Georgie," said the other Miss Postgate instructively, "has kindly consented to come and be our lady-cook."

Stacy gave a little jump. She wasn't aware of having actually done anything of the sort!

"Oh, that will be very nice!" Miss Georgie murmured vaguely. "When does she come?"

"I think we have hardly settled that yet, Georgie.—When *can* you come?" said the small Miss Postgate to Stacy, who found herself answering, in a rather bewildered fashion, that term ended next Thursday, and she could come—oh, any time after that!

"You will be able to come at once? You weren't thinking of taking a holiday first?"

Stacy said "Yes" to the first question, and then "No" to the second.

"That would be very convenient for us, as our cook has already left. Shall we say next Thursday, then—at about six o'clock?"

Stacy said "Yes" again. She was feeling more and more bewildered.

"Then that will suit us very well. Good-bye, Miss Wayland,

till next Thursday! And I hope we shall all get on very well together."

She held out her small thin hand, like a claw; and Miss Georgie held out hers, which was plump and warm and soft; and Stacy shook first one and then the other, and walked out of the house feeling rather as if she were walking in a dream. But not a nightmare—oh, no! She had *wanted* this job; she was very thankful to have secured it. If she could give satisfaction— and there seemed really no reason why she shouldn't—she was safely provided for, for the next year or two.

She looked round the roads and streets of Upper Galting, that eminently respectable suburb, and shuddered a little. A year or two—here! It seemed a tremendous piece out of a person's life. There rose up suddenly before her vision, unbidden, a big stately building, with jolly girls all about, on tennis courts and swimming in a big pool. …

She turned sharply into the station entrance, and went down the dirty stairs, and waited for a considerable time on the dirty platform, and got into the dirty suburban train. And so, eventually, she reached London proper once more, and stood waiting for her bus, telling herself fiercely that it would be wonderful to have all these gorgeous shops within easy distance, and theatres, and—oh, all the wonders of London, to see and enjoy at her leisure.

"*Stacy!*"

"Oh! Oh, hallo, Janet!" said Stacy, a good deal taken aback at the unexpected meeting, but very glad indeed to see any one—even Janet Tripp—who might turn her thoughts into a pleasanter channel.

Janet was very smart indeed and, as usual, very full of self-confidence. She told Stacy that if she walked to another corner, two minutes away, she would save a penny of her bus fare; and they went along together, talking. Janet was a full-fledged clerk now in her uncle's office. She had thoroughly enjoyed her secretarial training. Her fellow-clerks were most agreeable. She was earning thirty-five shillings a week. She had a good deal to say about all this; and there was nothing to prevent her, for Stacy was uncommonly silent.

"And what are *you* doing in London, Stacy?" Janet bethought herself to inquire, when they had reached the other corner and were waiting again. "You haven't left your College yet, have you? Oh, next week, is it? And what are you going to do then?"

"Oh, hallo, Janet!"

"I've just been seeing about a post," Stacy told her. (Oh, if it had *only* been that Dorset school! How different her voice would have been as she told about it; and how the whole thing would have impressed Janet.)

"Where? *Upper Galting?* Good heavens!"

Janet had very slightly better manners than Miss Smithkins. She didn't actually *say* that she wouldn't be seen dead in such a locality, but her voice and manner were almost equally eloquent.

"And what are you going to do there?"

"Cook!" said Stacy, with her head up.

"*Cook?*"

"Our Principal likes all of us to take a cooking job first, if possible. She says that, after that, we know everything there is to know about a kitchen; and it gives us such a strong position when we take a superior post."

"And how much …?" Janet began, her face working with curiosity. (After all, *she* had told her salary, and why shouldn't Stacy reciprocate?) But at that crucial moment the bus blessedly hove in sight, and Stacy swung herself quickly up, just calling out, "Good-bye! Nice to have seen you!" over the heads of the people who came after her. And she was borne away to her other terminus, and got thankfully into a clean main-line train, and so, very weary and not too cheerful, reached the pleasant haven of College once more. She had to tell Miss Pim all about it, of course, but that was soon over. The Principal was one of those rare people who never cry over spilt milk, or waste time in regretting what is absolutely settled. Stacy went back to her delightful little room that she had grown to love, and made up her mind sensibly to enjoy to the utmost these last few days in the place where she had been very happy.

CHAPTER VIII

Cook

STACY sent her box on as Luggage in Advance, so she had nothing to carry but the fascinating little zip-fastened suit-case that Agatha had given her, with its umbrella grip at the back. She started out on her journey with her mind made up to look at the bright side of things, and to make a marvellous success of her first job; and since it was a very fine April day, even Upper Galting looked its best. The bell and door-handle of Number Seventeen had been well cleaned since she saw them first, which in itself was a cheering sight. Miss Wilhelmina Postgate, opening the door, smiled at sight of her—rather a thin, tight-lipped smile, but still that was cheering too.

"I am glad to see you, Miss Wayland," she said. "Come in. Your box has already gone up to your room. I expect you will like to unpack and arrange your things at once."

"Yes, please," said Stacy.

"I will show you the way," said Miss Postgate.

There was not really any doubt about the way, since there was only one very narrow staircase, and the cook's room was, naturally, at the top of the house. Miss Postgate pointed out the door of her room, and the door of her sister's, and the bathroom door at the end, as she passed them. The last flight of stairs was covered with rather worn linoleum. On the landing at the top there were, again, three doors: a spare bedroom, a box-room, and Stacy's room.

"We very rarely have any visitor to stay. When we do, my sister moves up here and gives up her room," said Miss Postgate. "When you have unpacked your box, please put it in the box-room. I like to have everything tidied away at once."

She went downstairs again. Stacy turned the handle of the back bedroom and stood looking into it.

Well, she *was* only a cook after all, even though she was College trained; and it had to be remembered that all her predecessors here had only been the ordinary kind of cook— who did not, presumably, care whether the window opened or not. It was not open now, but Stacy soon saw to that—with a little difficulty, for it was stuck fast. Then she looked round again. There was a very narrow bed that looked lumpy, and the usual servant's furniture, painted in the usual unhappy pale grained paint to imitate natural wood: little chest of drawers, small washstand with a drawer underneath, one cane-seated chair. On the door there was one double hook. Otherwise there was no place to hang anything. The floor was of bare boards, with one strip of very well-worn carpet by the side of the bed. Stacy felt damped, until she caught sight of her reflection in the very little looking-glass that stood on the little chest of drawers, and then she burst out laughing—it was such a very bad piece of glass, that looking into it was like looking into one of those pestiferous mirrors beloved of the seaside tripper.

The view from the window was unexpectedly good: over little suburban gardens, walled away from each other, and, of course, more houses beyond, and a church with a really beautiful spire, and quite a lot of trees in the distance. Stacy decided that there must be some sort of public park or garden there. She would investigate on her first day out.

She began to unpack quickly, very much dashed again to find the drawers unlined and full of oddments, sweet-papers, dust, and broken beads. Mercifully she had a newspaper with her, and she used one sheet to collect all this unattractive debris, and neatly lined the drawers with the rest. Then she put her box in the box-room as directed, with her suit-case inside, washed her hands (which needed it badly) in a basin that was cracked and had a high-water mark, and went down, very neat and trim, in her College uniform of white overall and white cap.

Miss Postgate was waiting for her in the hall, glancing up with approval.

"Now I will show you the kitchen; but first—my sister and I do not know what to call you! 'Miss Wayland' sounds odd; and it is so long. What is your name?"

Stacy said, in the hard voice that always went with that painful confession, "My name is Anastasia."

Miss Postgate was waiting for her.

"Really! But that is longer still. Have you no other name?"

"I'm afraid not," said Stacy, wishing for the five-hundredth time that she had.

Miss Postgate meditated.

"We have always been accustomed to say 'Cook,'" she remarked in a tentative voice. "But perhaps you would not like? …"

"I don't mind in the least!" Stacy told her hastily. She would rather be Cook than Anastasia, any day.

"Oh, very well—if you really *don't* mind."

On the left of the front door there was an unobtrusive door, giving on to a staircase, of which Miss Postgate observed, most truly, that it was rather dark and narrow, and Stacy would need to be careful until she got used to it. Three or four doors opened off from a small lobby down below, and Stacy found herself looking round the kitchen almost immediately— rather small, moderately tidy, furnished with an old-fashioned coal range, a very large wooden table, a dresser set out with crockery, and two Windsor chairs. Nothing else. The window, which was a large bay, looked out on to a very small paved yard and up to the pavement, giving an excellent view of the feet and legs of passers-by.

"The scullery leads out on this side, and the larder on the other. You will find it all quite convenient," said Miss Postgate.

She directed Stacy's attention to a little collection of food set out under a wire cover on the table.

"Here is all that you will need for preparing supper. Cutlets, potatoes, and a custard pudding, please."

"Will you have the pudding cold or hot?" Stacy inquired, very business-like.

"Cold, please," said Miss Postgate with a gleam of approval. "Then you can bring it all up together, leaving the pudding and cold plates on the sideboard. We do not expect you to wait."

It had not occurred to Stacy that a cook would be expected

to wait at any time; but, of course, her College training had included parlour-work, so there was no difficulty about it.

"Keep one cutlet for yourself," Miss Postgate continued, "and, of course, you can finish the pudding when you bring it down. We will ring when we have finished. I expect my maids to go to bed not later than ten, and to be down in the morning by half-past six. Breakfast at half-past eight: tea, toast, and lightly boiled eggs. You will find all you need in the larder. Please take in a pint of milk in the morning. ... Now I will leave you to learn your way about."

She went out; and Stacy stoked her fire, as a good cook should, and then proceeded to look about her, turning up a disgusted nose at the scullery and deciding to give it what *she* called a thorough turn-out at the earliest opportunity. The coal-cellar was extremely small. The larder was extremely empty. Neatly stacked together were three eggs in a bowl, a very little tea in a tightly shut tin box, three lumps of sugar, and a very tiny pat of butter.

As Stacy stood observing these, a cautious footstep made her turn back to the kitchen. Miss Georgiana Postgate had come in on tiptoe, and was looking anxiously back to see if she had been followed.

"Oh, how do you do?" she said in a very low voice, holding out her hand. "*Do* you take sugar in your tea?"

Stacy, rather taken aback, said "Yes," and the round, pink, lined face opposite suddenly drooped like a disappointed child's.

"*Oh!*"

"Why?" Stacy inquired, not understanding.

"Well, if you didn't, you see, you could have *said* you did, and given it to me!"

"I couldn't possibly say I did if I didn't," Stacy told her with firmness.

"Oh," said Miss Georgie again, "that's a pity. If you do

things like that I'm afraid you'll be rather hungry. ... What's for breakfast?"

Stacy showed her.

"Eggs again! ... But of course it would be eggs; they're cheap just now. Sometimes," said Miss Georgie in a luscious voice, "we have *sausages*. But not very often, of course. ... Do you mind beetles?"

"I *loathe* them," said Stacy in no uncertain tone.

"Oh, that's a pity," said Miss Georgie, "because I'm afraid there are rather a lot. ... Was that one there—by the fender?"

Stacy turned sharply. But there was no beetle. On the other hand, there were only two lumps of sugar in the little bowl where there had previously been three. Miss Georgie, rather crowding her out of the larder into the kitchen, was slightly pinker than before.

"You needn't try to open that cupboard," she said, hastily turning the subject, "because it's locked. Willie—my sister, Miss Wilhelmina, I mean—always keeps it locked. She'll give you out what you want in the morning. ... *What* did you say your name was?"

Stacy told her in the cold averse tone kept for that distasteful confession, which seemed rather to alarm Miss Georgie.

"I heard Willie—Miss Wilhelmina—ask you, because the drawing-door was a little open when you came downstairs, but I wasn't sure. What a wonderful name! How do you spell it?"

Stacy spelt it, but Miss Georgie, listening with her head on one side, was not satisfied.

"Please write it down," she requested. "It's a *wonderful* name, and I never heard it before. And you haven't any other?"

Stacy shook her head. She was writing as directed, with a pencil from her pocket, on a small edge of newspaper that seemed the only thing available.

"Thank you," said Miss Georgie, taking it from her and scanning it carefully. "Would you mind if I called you by it sometimes when we are quite alone? I know we are calling you Cook, in a general way."

Stacy did mind, but she had not the heart to say so if the concession was likely to give pleasure in what seemed likely to be a rather unpleasurable life.

"Oh, *thank* you! … There's Willie going upstairs. I must fly!"

Flat-footed elderly people are not apt to fly in a very fairy-like manner, but Miss Georgie certainly slipped up the dark kitchen stairs with much rapidity and very little noise in a manner which spoke of long practice. Stacy looked at the flat-faced kitchen clock, and looked again at her fire, and decided that it was time to begin supper preparations—a little distraught because there was no extra egg available for the elegant bread-crumbing of her cutlets. But she did the best she could without it; and presumably her efforts were successful, for she heard nothing more of her mistresses that night. She ate her supper a little forlornly and without much appetite, and went to bed soon after without waiting for ten o'clock. It *was* lonely; and she did hate beetles extremely, and had no wish to wait up until they began their nocturnal revels. Besides, a Windsor chair offers no inducements in the way of rest; and she had nothing to read except the very few books of her own that she had brought with her.

She had served, and cleared away, and washed up breakfast next morning before the arrival of Mrs. Blott, the daily servant who did not wish to live in. And Stacy did not take long in deciding that she herself was glad of this decision. Mrs. Blott was a long lean lady with a long yellow face, and she had no conversation whatsoever. She greeted Stacy with a bleak stare, collected what she needed in the way of brooms and dustpans and the like, and departed upstairs on her trivial round, while Stacy learned the meaning of Miss Georgie's cryptic remarks about the locked cupboard. It was the frugal habit of Miss

Wilhelrnina, after ordering meals for the day, to weigh out
with her own hands all that was necessary for cooking—so
much rice, so much sugar, so much margarine and butter and
dripping, so much flour—and subsequently to lock up all that
remained and go upstairs again for the day. Nothing was left to
Stacy's discretion except the milk and the bread, and she was
very distinctly told how much to order of both. Meat came
in—a very little joint of neck of mutton—and at luncheon
time her portion was cut off and given out to her. Even the
potatoes were duly counted, allowing two per head. A small
pot of jam, she was explicitly informed, was supposed to last
her for a week. Tea was given out in spoonfuls, cheese was
treated as if it were made of gold, three rashers of bacon
(for next morning's breakfast) were placed reverentially on a
plate by themselves. Stacy began to realize—having recovered
her natural fine appetite after a sound night's rest on a rather
hard flock pillow—that Miss Georgie had not been speaking
without warrant when she suggested the possibility of hunger.

She learned this more clearly still when a sudden
unseasonable spell of very hot weather tainted the very small
joint that had already done duty for two days, once hot and
once cold. Miss Postgate had decided that it would last out for
one more day as a potato pie; and, when her reluctant nose
agreed with the verdict of Stacy's nose, she was by no means
prepared to go to unexpected expense. The meat *ought* to have
lasted for a third day. Its failing to do so was a misfortune, but
not a justification for further expense. She served out, with
manifest reluctance, a small extra ration of cheese; and Stacy,
that day happening to be her day out, bought two large new
penny buns and was sorry when they were finished. She came
in to find Miss Georgie prowling stealthily round the kitchen
and larder with a hungry and disappointed expression. The
three lumps of sugar, doled out for next morning's tea, had
vanished.

"Yes, I did eat them, Anastasia—I'm sorry!" said Miss Georgie, like a child found out in its fault. "I was so hungry!"

"It doesn't matter," Stacy soothed her. She was genuinely sorry for the poor thing, who had such a passionate love for everything sweet, and so little chance to gratify it. Apparently Miss Postgate kept the family purse in her own hands, and kept the strings tightly drawn.

As if she had followed this train of thought, Miss Georgie sat down in one of the Windsor chairs, folded her soft, plump hands on the table, and spoke freely.

"My sister Willie manages all our money affairs, you know, Anastasia."

"Oh!" said Stacy discreetly.

"She's a very *good* manager!" said Miss Georgie loyally.

"I am sure she is," said Stacy.

"And I should be no good at all. I never could do sums," Miss Georgie confessed openly. "But I can't help sometimes wishing, Anastasia, that *she* liked nice things to eat—as I do. And you do too, don't you?"

"Very much indeed," said Stacy.

"When our parents died—oh, a great many years ago," said Miss Georgie, "Willie and I made our wills, of course, leaving everything to each other."

She looked cautiously round, drew nearer, and spoke in a lowered voice.

"Willie is much older than I am, you know. Of course, I hope that she will live for a long, long time! I can't think how I should get on without her. But if she does die first, do you know what I shall do?"

Stacy shook her head, not at all sure whether she ought to encourage these alarming confidences.

"I shall have a Real Feast!" said Miss Georgie, opening her large pale eyes very wide with an eager and excited expression. "I do hope it's not wrong of me to think of it. I am very fond of Willie, but, of course, she *is* much older than I am. And I do think of it quite often, especially when I feel hungry in bed. ... I expect I shall feel hungry to-night, after no meat, you know."

Stacy felt remorseful about her buns, but that was of no use now.

"I'll tell you just what I shall have," said Miss Georgie, closing her eyes as if in an ecstatic dream. "I shall have first, rich, thick white soup—the kind that you make with cream. Then I shall have a turkey, roast, with two sorts of stuffing—chestnut

"I shall have a Real Feast!" said Miss Georgie.

and the other—and sausages round, lots of sausages—*pork*
sausages. And roast potatoes. And green peas. But when I
come to the pudding I never *can* make up my mind!"

"Why not?" Stacy inquired, feeling quiet hungry again at
the mere mention of all this embarrassment of riches.

"Well," said Miss Georgie seriously, "it would certainly be
either trifle *or* meringues; but they are both so good, and *I can't*
decide. Do you—do you think it would be very greedy to have
both?"

Stacy shook her head. It was a little difficult not to smile at
the extreme earnestness of the question.

"Really not? Then I *should* have both!" said Miss Georgie
triumphantly, as if her mind were relieved of a great weight.
"And then, of course, dessert—figs, and dates, and almonds
and raisins, and crystallized fruits …"

"Georgie, can you possibly be in the kitchen?" a voice
called from upstairs.

Miss Georgie started up with guilt and great haste.

"Yes, Willie, yes! I was just saying goodnight to Cook. It is
so lonely for her to come in and find no one to speak to!"

She vanished in her soft-footed, circumspect fashion,
turning at the door to put her finger to her lip, in the manner
of a very old-fashioned actress, as a sign of caution to Stacy,
who went to bed, there being no reason for staying up any
longer, but found it hard to sleep—perhaps because, as Miss
Georgie had suggested, she was hungry. Visions kept dancing
before her unwilling eyes of a delightful bed-sitting room with
comfortable chairs, of wide grounds with girls walking and
playing in them, of a great, spacious, well-found kitchen where
the cooking staff for ever dished up meals that were simple,
of course—one would expect nothing else in a school—but
plentiful, and pleasing to the eye, and pleasant to the taste. …
Stacy, tossing and turning on her lumpy bed, sternly banished
these too-pleasing dreams again and again, but they kept on

recurring. She fell asleep finally with one firm determination in her mind—if she were ever again, as seemed too probable, driven to supplement Miss Willie's meagre rations, she would not fail to bring in a similar supplement for poor Miss Georgie.

CHAPTER IX

Work and Play

PRESUMABLY Stacy's first week at Number Seventeen consisted, in the usual way, of seven days; but it felt more like a year. After that, however, she began to grow acclimatized to her new life, and time went at a rather more normal rate. Her position was lonely, of course; but she had to make up her mind to that. The servants in neighbouring houses made one or two tentative efforts at friendliness, but as she was forbidden to ask them in, and as she found them far from congenial, that soon fell through. Miss Georgie paid a good many surreptitious visits to the kitchen, and Stacy's feeling for her advanced from pity to a queer sort of affection. She was a very simple soul, of course, and her love of sweet things was babyish; but apart from that she was shrewd enough, and her comments were often oddly amusing. She was certainly fond of Stacy; and she was childishly grateful for an occasional very small present of cake or sweets. Stacy would have loved to bring something in with her every time she went out, but funds forbade—one has to be uncommonly careful with thirty pounds a year (less insurance stamps) when it must cover clothing and holidays and all incidental expenses.

She found at first that so much confinement to the house was extremely trying, for Miss Postgate was of the old school who considered two outings a week more than enough for any young servant. Stacy, accustomed to plenty of air and exercise both at school and at college, felt rather like a bird in a small and stuffy cage. But there it was; she had got to get used to it, like many other things; and she made occasion, whenever both her ladies were out, to walk briskly round and round the small formal garden at the back, which was a little (if not much) better than nothing. She made the most, too, of her two weekly half-days, going for long walks and exploring the neighbourhood thoroughly. It wasn't too bad a suburb after all, if one was determined to make the best of it. Those *were* public gardens whose trees she could see from her bedroom window: very stiff and uninteresting, but at least free from houses, and with seats where one could rest and look about one. So she quickly grew accustomed to her very limited leisure—and perhaps, in one way, it was all for the best, for she found herself with an unpleasantly sharpened appetite after these biweekly excursions. Miss Postgate, who meant very well indeed, would have been horrified beyond measure if any one had accused her of starving her servants. It never occurred to her for a moment that a big girl of nineteen required more to eat than a little thin woman in her sixties.

There came twice to the house, for two morning hours, a charwoman who did rough work—not too efficiently in Stacy's critical estimation. There was no love lost between her and Mrs. Porges, who was gifted with a long tongue, and would have liked to exercise it without ceasing as she scrubbed. As for Mrs. Blott the daily servant, Stacy got very little farther with her, for the exactly opposite reason, for she was the most silent and unapproachable of women. But she had a little boy who was badly crippled, and who used to swing himself along on his crutches towards six o'clock and stand patiently waiting for his mother—whom he obviously adored—until she was free to come out and go home with him. It hurt Stacy badly to see him standing there, shifting wearily from one foot to the other. She made bold to ask Miss Postgate if in this one instance the rule about kitchen visitors might be broken, and met with a stiff and astonished refusal.

"A little boy in *my* kitchen? Certainly not, Cook! He would do endless mischief; and possibly he might not even be honest!"

There was little, Stacy thought to herself, that any boy would care to carry away out of the Postgate kitchen; but she only said mildly that she did not think he would do any mischief. He looked a very quiet little boy, and he was too badly crippled to move about with ease.

"*All* boys do mischief!" said Miss Postgate, and closed the interview with decision. Obviously nothing was to be gained by reopening the question.

The silent Mrs. Blott broke her silence for once to thank Stacy for her effort.

"But it ain't no use; I'd asked meself. Billy do get tired standing there, but he just *will* come and wait for me. There's only the two of us, you see."

When Stacy was paid her wages she broke into that cherished sum to buy Billy a little present. Nothing much, only a highly coloured picture-book full of pictures of trains. But it gave Billy immense pleasure, and his mother also. And on Stacy's next day out she found her way with some difficulty to the unattractive little street where Mrs. Blott lived, and took a bag of buns with her—instead of buying herself a very frugal tea as usual—and shared them with Billy. It was not very far from the public gardens that she had discovered; and she took him there afterwards, seeing him carefully across two roads which he was forbidden to cross alone; and found it quite painful to hear his raptures. Crikey, what flowers them was in the beds! Wasn't they bright, just! Yes, Mum did bring him here now and then of a Sunday; but gen'ly her bad leg made her glad just to lie and rest like, on the bed. ... Stacy repeated the little expedition more than once, on fine days; but it happened to be a late and cold spring, and there were many days suitable only for a quick, warming walk, impossible to a small cripple. ... Mrs. Blott said nothing, but Stacy found one or two distasteful oddments of work done for her when she came in—it made that rather desolate return less chilling than it had ever been.

She went once, by invitation, to tea with Janet, meeting her by appointment after City offices were closed.

"How thin you've got, Stacy!" was Janet's greeting.

"Good!" said Stacy with a laugh.

She felt very shabby, comparing her own clothes with Janet's smart new coat and skirt, of exactly the shade of green that she shouldn't have worn—she had always had execrable taste in dress. Stacy hoped that it wasn't spiteful to observe how very unbecoming it was.

"You look as if you didn't get enough to eat!" said Janet, whose sharp eyes had always been noted for seeing everything. She looked rather uncomfortable and alarmed as she spoke; and Stacy, who had been looking forward to her tea, made up her mind there and then to eat as little as was humanly possible—generosity had never been Janet's strong suit. It was difficult to do this when it came to the point, for the smell and sight of plentiful food was terribly tempting; but she kept herself well in hand, only choosing plain and filling food that would go as far as possible.

"But you always used to *like* cake!" said Janet with a relieved but surprised glance as Stacy refused a sugary trifle that made her mouth water and chose instead a very stodgy scone.

"So I do, but I'd rather have this to-day, thank you."

"Oh, well! Of course, if you're not feeling *well*," said Janet, not pressing the matter, for the scone was very much cheaper than the sugar-cake. And Stacy allowed her to suppose that if she chose, hoping that it was not an unspoken lie.

"Have you heard anything of Agatha?"

Stacy didn't say that she heard from Agatha every week. She only related how Sir Humphrey had, at last, bought an English house—or rather a Welsh one, just over the border—and that he and Agatha were having a delightful time choosing furniture before they settled in.

"Have you heard anything of Agatha?"

"And I suppose you'll be asked to stay there as soon as they do!" said Janet with envy.

"I can't go anywhere till I get my holiday; and I don't know when that will be," was Stacy's pacific answer. She knew perfectly well (for Sir Humphrey had been extremely outspoken on the subject) that Janet was no more likely to be invited than Mrs. Blott. Out of kindness, she would not for anything have told Janet that she herself had a standing invitation to go as often, and stay as long, as she liked.

"I suppose you won't get *much* holiday, anyhow," said Janet.

"Not more than a fortnight at the most," said Stacy.

"Do you really *like* being a cook?" Janet inquired, half curious and half patronizing.

"I always did like cooking," said Stacy. "But I do hope, later on, to get a job where I'll get more practice with more difficult things—or I'll forget so much. Of course, it is just as well to begin with something simple."

Janet was not really interested in the subject at all. She went on quickly to what did interest her extremely: her own office, and her fellow-clerks, and what a pull it gave her to be the niece of the firm, and what fun she had in the evenings, and how jolly it was to be free for half Saturday and all Sunday. She didn't find the work hard—oh, dear, no! And it was topping to have thirty-five shillings a week of her very own. Of course (very loftily), she felt it only fair to pay ten shillings of that to her mother, as she lived at home and they weren't very rich; and, of course, there were bus fares and that sort of thing. But it was really quite a good beginning; and, of course, presently she'd get a rise …

And so on, and so on. Stacy didn't find it all particularly interesting—Janet's conversation rarely was—but she was quite content to sit still, and listen, and rest. It was lovely to have a sufficient meal that had cost her nothing, and to know that somebody else would have to wash up.

"Well, we must meet again some time," said Janet, rising at last.

"Rather!" said Stacy, knowing, with a sinking of heart, that on that occasion it would be her turn to play hostess. She had successfully avoided owning to the smallness of her salary; and, in any case, Janet was the sort of person who demanded chicken for chicken.

"I'm afraid we'll have to part now," said Janet, looking at a new and impressive wristwatch. "I'm going out to bridge and supper, and I'll only just have time to get home and dress."

Stacy politely hoped that she would have a good time. Janet was emphatically *sure* that she would, and they separated. As a matter of fact, neither was terribly keen to repeat the meeting.

It was a couple of weeks after that that Miss Postgate suddenly told Stacy she could take a week of her holiday almost immediately. They had had an invitation to go and stay with old friends, and she proposed to shut up the house during their absence. She did not inquire whether Stacy had anywhere to go at such short notice; she had, as a matter of fact, never made any inquiry at all about her young cook's private life. If there had not been that always-open invitation, Stacy would have found herself awkwardly placed, since she had hardly saved enough to provide for a week's board and lodging—shoes had had to be bought, and one or two other dull necessaries. She would just have enough for a return ticket to Agatha's new home, and that was all. … What a wonderful thing it was to send a hasty note announcing her holiday, and to receive a warm telegram of pleasure early next morning!

Miss Postgate was a little exercised about that telegram. She took it in herself, seeing the boy coming up the steps, and rang the bell for Stacy with something not far removed from displeasure.

"A *telegram* for you, Cook!"

"I expect it is from the friends to whom I am going," said Stacy, pink and bright eyed.

"You had better open it. It may be a mistake."

Stacy obeyed; and it was not a mistake; and she said so.

"By the way," Miss Postgate added as an afterthought, "you had better give me your address. I *might* need to write to you— if we decided to return unexpectedly early, for instance."

Devoutly hoping that that decision would not be made, Stacy obediently wrote down Sir Humphrey Phayre's new address, at which Miss Postgate looked with raised eyebrows. She had never forgotten, of course, the mention of that well-known name during her initial interview with Stacy, but she had never quite brought herself to believe that it was more than a flourish of trumpets. There was something more than surprise in her tone as she dismissed Stacy to the kitchen.

Miss Georgie was openly overjoyed at the prospect of her holiday, fairly bubbling over when she told Stacy so.

"Is it a pretty place?" Stacy inquired politely.

"Oh, yes; at least, I suppose so. All places are a good deal alike, don't you think? But the Perrings give one such *lovely* food, and so much of it! ... I do hope, Anastasia," she added with an anxious, kind afterthought, "that *you* will be well fed where you are going?"

"Yes, indeed!" Stacy assured her, smiling irrepressibly at the contrast between Miss Postgate's idea of a dinner and Sir Humphrey's.

"*That's* all right, then!" said Miss Georgie, completely satisfied, and wanting to know nothing further.

Mrs. Blott, on the other hand, had received her intimation of a holiday in a silent gloom of dismay. She even went the length of telling Stacy, in an unusual burst of confidence, that she did not expect to get any temporary job for so short a time, and that Miss Postgate never paid her any sort of retaining fee on such occasions.

"But what will you *do*, Mrs. Blott?" Stacy asked, aghast. She had already learned the vital importance of a steady wage when one has no private resources to back it up.

"Do? What we've done afore!" said Mrs. Blott grimly, and relapsed into her customary taciturnity.

It almost spoilt the brightness of Stacy's expectations. (As a matter of fact, she related the incident to Agatha very soon after her arrival, which resulted in the dispatch of a generous money-order, and Mrs. Blott's bursting into tears on the receipt of it, and Billy's going to the seaside for a whole long day for the very first time in his life.) But nothing could really do that! It was too wonderful to get out of the house early in the morning—she had almost forgotten what morning sunshine feels like—and sit at ease first in a bus and then in a suburban train, with no damping prospect of a return journey that same evening; and subsequently to travel fast and luxuriously, leaving first the suburbs behind, and then the Midlands, and finally to see the Welsh hills welcoming her. And, best of all, to look out at Agatha's beloved and lovely face, smiling up at her from the platform of a very little country station.

"This is not the same chauffeur," Stacy remarked when their first raptures were over and they were rolling fast and smoothly along steeply rising roads.

"Of course not," Agatha smiled at her. "Barkis belonged to the house where we were last time."

"Oh, of course! Do you like your new house as well?"

"Oh, ever so much better!" Agatha assured her eagerly. "First because it is our very own; and then because it isn't so enormous—we didn't want a huge place like that when we really settled down."

And, certainly, when they came to it, the new house proved to be nothing like so big, though it was a huge mansion when compared with Number Seventeen St. Philibert's Terrace; and Stacy agreed with Agatha that it was all the pleasanter. In a much more modest way, the gardens were quite delightful; and if there was only one tennis court—well, as Agatha said, in that western county they had so much rain that a hard one was very much more useful than grass. The servants, also, were fewer and less terrific; though it seemed to Stacy, fresh from the rigours of Miss Postgate, that they did very much as they pleased about everything. Agatha certainly went through some farce of seeing the cook every morning; but as for "giving orders," Stacy roundly taxed her with never doing anything of the sort.

"Well, why should I?" Agatha smiled at her. "Mrs. Sargent

knows everything, and I know nothing—and she knows that quite well too."

Stacy had a vaguely uncomfortable feeling that there was something wrong about this, but she contented herself with asking Agatha what she would do if the all-knowing one chose to leave.

"Why, get some one as much like her as possible, of course, as fast as possible!" said Agatha comfortably. "Come along, Stacy, and I'll show you our very best view."

They had to climb pretty steeply for half an hour to get there, but the result was well worth it. Stacy, gazing rapturously in one direction after another—all so gloriously different from Upper Galting—suddenly made a discovery.

"Agatha, haven't I been here before?"

Agatha gave one of her happy, soft laughs.

"I was wondering when you'd find it out! Don't you remember that absurd drive of ours, when we went just where we thought we'd like to, and the car broke down? We passed quite close to this house then. Wouldn't it have been thrilling if we'd known that?"

"Then that is Chapel Cloud!" Stacy cried triumphantly, pointing to a high-standing church just across a narrow valley.

Agatha turned an agreeable pink.

"Yes. We're just at the very edge of the parish."

"Then you go to church there?"

"Well, of course!"

"How is Mr. Blount?" Stacy inquired in a carefully careless tone, looking tactfully at the view. And Agatha replied, in an exactly similar tone, that he was very well, and came quite often to tennis. Sir Humphrey liked him very much.

If there was one thing about this delightful visit that was vaguely less pleasant than the first, it was in some unknown way connected with Sir Humphrey. Perhaps he was not quite well, though he certainly looked as fit as possible. Perhaps he found it trying to be securely anchored in England at last after so many years of wandering. Perhaps, after that perfectly free life, he found the inevitable worries of a household a little irksome. Certainly he seemed very much to resent the many letters that beset his plate at breakfast-time—even to the extent of throwing a good many of them, unopened, into the waste-paper basket that was always put beside him. Whatever the cause of this undefined annoyance, it had nothing to do with Agatha which very much relieved Stacy, because she had at first connected it with some idea of Mr. Blount or other

"Then that is Chapel Cloud!"

like offenders; but the manner of father and daughter towards each other was, as always, perfect. Agatha repeated more than once, for Stacy's benefit, with a good deal of emphasis, that she had never met any man who compared for a moment with her father. Sir Humphrey, even more openly, challenged Stacy to say that any girl in the neighbourhood—or elsewhere, for that matter—could hold a candle to Agatha, which met always with a whole-hearted assent.

The glorious week was filled as full as it could hold with tennis, picnics, and all country delights; and Stacy went back, brown and rosy and quite definitely fatter, with a new hand-bag which she was under solemn bond not to open until she was in the train (it proved to contain five pounds in a purse, with the sweetest of messages begging her not to be offended) and an immense basket of strawberries, which cost her the expense of a porter at every station and nearly broke her arm as she lugged it from the bus to St. Philibert's Terrace. But that was nothing compared with the childish joy of Miss Georgie at sight of it, and the unchildlike awe of Billy Blott when he was given his share. He hadn't never seen them things, except in winders—and never that big, and never that red and shining.

CHAPTER X

GUILD MEETING

AS spring turned to summer, one feeling, one wish, one fear filled Stacy's mind—would it be possible that she might be spared to go to the College Guild meeting? She had managed to pay her life subscription with infinite difficulty out of her very slender means, because it was the thing of all others nearest her heart. To stay in Upper Galting while it was going on would be purgatory. To go would be—well, simply marvellous! No other words could describe it. The College had no greater testimony than this fact that, in spite of working its students hard and keeping them under pretty strict control, their only thought was to fly back there, like homing pigeons, at every available opportunity.

Stacy's dreams, by night and day, were filled with the joys of meeting old friends, hearing all the news, revisiting old haunts, seeing Miss Pim—a terror as well as a joy, this last. But—would Miss Postgate ever consent? It seemed very far from likely.

She took her bull by the horns at last, and made her desperate petition. She would gladly get up at any unearthly hour on that Saturday morning, doing beforehand all possible work, and leave everything in apple-pie order. She would return without fail on Sunday night. She waited, breathless, for the life-and-death verdict.

Miss Postgate was struck dumb. No former cook, she explained on recovering her breath, had ever suggested anything so unheard-of. She was surprised; astonished, in fact.

"Especially, Cook, as you have just *had* a week's holiday! It is really a most extraordinary request."

Stacy wanted to point out that that week's holiday had

been forced upon her whether she liked it or not, without any consideration at all of whether the time suited her, or any previous warning, but she held her tongue. She wanted so desperately to go! No other subsequent Guild meeting could ever again be like this one, the first after leaving College: when she was sure of meeting her own contemporaries, who would be equally anxious to discuss old times (three or four months ago, but already feeling years away), to compare notes of the present, to sympathize with anticipations of the future.

"It is really," Miss Postgate was continuing acidly, "a *most* extraordinary thing to ask, so soon, for two days to which you have no possible right."

"Only a day and a half," Stacy pleaded. "I should have been out on Sunday afternoon and evening, anyhow."

"A day and a half, then. How do you propose to make that up?"

"I'd do anything; absolutely anything you liked! You see …"

Stacy proceeded to explain the position; Miss Postgate listening coldly without the least real understanding. College life of any sort had never come into the scheme of her own youth. Stacy's words seemed to fall into a dreadful cold vacuum, and she herself began to grow cold with fright. Could Miss Postgate actually be thinking of dismissing her for such a daring request? She *couldn't*! If she did …

As a matter of fact, Miss Postgate was considering how best to turn this unexpected piece of audacity to her own profit. She had not the slightest intention of parting with Stacy; she knew when she had made a good bargain, and Stacy was a very good bargain. But it was her habit to extort the uttermost farthing, and she was now considering the best way of doing this. The girl was, obviously, so very eager that she would consent to anything; even, probably, to giving up the rest of the holiday that was still due to her. But that was unlikely to suit Miss Postgate herself, who was in the habit of going for a regulation fortnight to the seaside every summer with her sister, shutting up the house and disbanding her staff. There was, of course, another and most convenient plan …

"The only way in which you could possibly make up the time that is really mine," she said at last, speaking very slowly, "would be to give up all your free time until you go away for this week-end."

"Oh, I would gladly do that!" Stacy cried eagerly—too eagerly. Miss Postgate, seeing her enthusiasm, made the most of it.

"Even that," she pointed out, "would not make up for the inconvenience caused by your absence."

"I … I suppose not," Stacy admitted, crushed.

There was another disintegrating pause, for Miss Postgate was one of those rare women who know the value and the effect of silence.

"It is a little more than a month to the date you mention," she said at last, Stacy hanging upon every slow word with a tortured eagerness. "If you were willing to give up all your free time during that month, I … *might* consent."

"You mean—not go out at all?"

"Certainly not. That would be bad for your health," said Miss Postgate judicially. "Also, I should disapprove of your not going to church. You could go to one service on the Sundays, leaving this house when the bells began to ring and returning *at once*. Also, I would occasionally send you out on week-days to do errands for me; but you would have no *free* time."

It sounded a pretty grim prospect for more than a whole month, but Stacy was perhaps unduly thankful for small mercies. She thanked Miss Postgate warmly, and said that she was perfectly willing to agree to all that; and she was *very* much obliged to her, and it was so kind …

"Very well, then," said Miss Postgate, clinching the bargain before there was any time for reconsideration. "Then that is settled—for this once *only*. You must not expect any such concession again."

"Oh, *no*! And thank you *very* much," said Stacy fervently. The proposed arrangement had been put before her so ingeniously that she really felt as if she had a great deal to be thankful for. As for never expecting any such concession again—well, a year is an immense time at nineteen, and it would be a whole year before there was another Guild meeting! Perhaps she might not want to go quite so terribly then. Perhaps, even, she might have left Miss Postgate, though Miss Pim *did* like her students to keep their first posts for two years if possible. At any rate, sufficient to the day is the good, as well as the evil.

It proved, in practice, that her loss of all free time was very much harder to bear than she had expected; and a month is a long time. Stacy had never realized how much she had grown to value those two half-days a week, when she was free to do what she pleased and go where the fancy took her. Miss Postgate's errands were few and far between, and she expected them to be done in a moment of time. It seemed to the worried Stacy, waiting in a crowded shop or held up at a crossing by unceasing traffic, that her mistress must sit watch in hand while she was gone, timing her return by seconds. On each of the five Sundays she was expected to go to the church nearest at hand; partly because of that, and partly because the very High Church service was so short. Stacy, who had been brought up Low, hated it with all her might, but she was given no choice. St. Philibert's was in the same road. St. Jude's, where she usually went, was ten minutes away. St. Philibert's, therefore, it had to be; and if the smell of incense made her feel sick, so much the worse for her.

All this was trying; but one thing cut her to the heart, and that was Billy Blott. No more slow, halting excursions with him to the gardens, no more running in to see him at home if the weather were unfavourable. Stacy explained most fully to his mother how the land lay (Mrs. Blott took her explanation in absolute silence, saying no word good or bad) and sent him tiny presents, with promises to come again the very moment she had her next free time. She hoped anxiously that her messages were given, and that he was old enough to understand; but she minded for him a great deal more than for herself.

The end of the month was very hot indeed; it seemed to crawl as slowly as the fat bloated bluebottles that disgusted her at her work. She bought a fly-flapper—which Miss Postgate refused to provide as an unnecessary extravagance—and waged vindictive war in kitchen and larder, toiling wearily up at night to her hot and breathless little room, which seemed to absorb all the heat from the slated roof just above. ... But all this could be borne, since she was going to the Guild meeting. She made an absurd date-calendar, as if she had been a small child, and scratched off a black square every morning and a white square every night.

And the slow sands of that interminable month trickled out, and there were only three days more to run.

It seemed to Stacy that she had never known any days so hot and wearisome, any nights so broken and breathless. She lay awake counting the hours as they struck on the too-near clock of St. Philibert's, trying not to think of the swimming pool and the shady trees at that Dorset school (the tennis courts were no longer a temptation: she was too tired) and the cool breezes blowing up and down Agatha's Welsh hills and valleys. Her worst moments were those in which terrifying visions occurred to her of being taken ill, so that she was unable to go, or of one or both of the Misses Postgate falling ill, in their turn preventing her from going. It seemed to her that either of those contingencies would be quite unbearable.

Nothing in that weather could have been less attractive than the hot kitchen (Miss Postgate considered a gas-ring an extravagance, as it would be infallibly used at the same time as the range-fire) except the horrors of the larder. Milk soured in spite of the smallness of the quantity taken in and the most cunning devices of Stacy to keep it sweet. Fish was an offence to nose and hand, butcher's meat only less so. Let Stacy scrub until her hands were sore, flies and wasps seemed to find eatable scraps everywhere. Miss Postgate's food ideas were old-fashioned and rigid. Salads? Rabbit-food! Cold cheeish savouries were only suitable for gentlemen: ladies must *always* have sweet puddings. And who had ever heard of serving up cold cooked vegetables in any form? Yes, they might possibly *look* nice; but she had never found any such recipes in any cookery book whatsoever. As for American cereals, and American baked beans—well, they *were* American, and therefore quite unsuited to English tables. Tinned foods were notoriously unhealthy, even dangerous. Tongues in glass moulds were just permissible, but far too expensive for ordinary household consumption.

So Stacy baked and boiled, and stewed and fried, as if it had been December; and on the Friday she roasted a small leg of lamb, which Miss Postgate opined, in a martyred manner, would keep them going until her return. By that time Stacy's sense of smell had been so continuously offended that she could not say whether it was her fancy or not that the meat smelt tainted. Mrs. Blott, appealed to, said that it was all right. Miss Postgate refused offendedly even to look at it. It was not *her* business to decide that sort of point; and in any case she had always found her butcher most trustworthy and a man of experience—not, as she very plainly intimated, a fanciful girl who knew little. She went out to a parish meeting in the full heat of the sun at two o'clock, and perhaps it was not too wonderful that her temper was not at its best.

Stacy was busy tidying her kitchen for the afternoon when the front-door bell rang; and, as Mrs. Blott had not returned from her dinner, she ran up to answer it. A very tall man with rather a stern, grim face asked for Miss Georgiana Postgate. Yes, she was at home, said Stacy; and what name, please?

"Mr. Harbinger."

As Stacy hesitated over the name he suddenly smiled at her: such an unexpectedly pleasant smile that his face was no longer grim, or even stern, and he appeared quite young.

"You never knew that there was such a name, did you?"

He spelt it for her; and Stacy had a dim, vague remembrance of having seen it somewhere without taking much notice, on a brass plate. By that time she had shown him in, and Miss

He spelt it for her.

Georgie, in a flutter of what seemed to be mingled pleasure and alarm, was rising hurriedly to greet him.

"Oh, Mr. Harbinger! But I expected …"

"My uncle is away …" Stacy heard him saying as she closed the door. She laughed to herself, going down the dangerous kitchen stairs, at a fancy that Miss Georgie was quite pleased to see a young man instead of an old one. After all, it was very seldom that anything young came to that house!

She went on with her tidying; and when he left, quite a considerable time later, it was Mrs. Blott who let him out of the front door.

And now the last but one of the black squares was crossed off her calendar, and it was only a matter of hours before she started on her marvellous expedition. Miss Georgie came tiptoeing, in her stealthy way, into the kitchen, to say very kindly that she was so glad for Stacy to have the pleasure, and she did hope it would keep fine, and Stacy wasn't to worry about leaving her work. "You've left everything *beautiful*," said Miss Georgie, walking admiringly round the larder (and incidentally, as appeared later, taking two of Stacy's three lumps of sugar). Her manner was very odd: triumphant, alarmed, sly. She kept looking at Stacy and breaking into little unexplained gurgles of laughter. And then she observed Miss Postgate's well-known legs passing the kitchen window, and fled alarmedly upstairs again before the latch-key clicked in the front door.

It was terribly hot, so hot that Stacy felt almost sick when she went up to her baking attic room—but then, she had not been able to bring herself to eat any supper at all, which perhaps accounted for it. Miss Postgate had a perverse habit of ignoring times and seasons and climatic conditions, and she had chosen sausages as a suitable supper for this hot night— beef sausages, needless to say. In Stacy's opinion, they looked and smelt and felt revolting; and in any case, by the time she had prepared and cooked and sent up any meat dish in this weather she never wanted to touch it again. It was perhaps therefore hunger, as well as heat and excitement, which made her sleep so badly; and dawn found her up, triumphantly crossing off the last of her calendar squares.

It had been arranged, after a little difficulty, that she might dish up breakfast and then go off at once, leaving Mrs. Blott to clear away and wash up. And so she did; and flew upstairs for her hat and coat and Agatha's suit-case, and was out of the house before either of her ladies had appeared. Strictly speaking, she felt a little guilty; for Miss Postgate was the soul of punctuality—and perhaps the gong *had* rung two minutes before its appointed time!

It was not until she was safely in her express train, speeding away out of London, that she felt free to draw a long breath and consider herself safe. She had an absurd feeling that Miss Postgate's arm was long enough, anywhere on the south side of the river, to reach her and bring her back.

CHAPTER XI

ALL OVER

IT is not often, in this disappointing world, that a holiday comes quite up to expectation, therefore Stacy was exceedingly lucky to find hers everything—perhaps more than everything—that she had hoped of it. The all-pervading sense of unaccustomed freedom was in itself a joy. The weather was perfect. She was put up at her own old hostel, and she met just the people whom she wanted to meet. Miss Pim was more than gracious: very nearly affectionate. She looked at Stacy with that all-penetrating glance of hers, and then asked hardly any questions at all except, "Getting on well, Miss Wayland?" And Stacy bravely answered that she was getting on perfectly well, and did not find the work too hard, and that Upper Galting was a more interesting place than she had supposed. Miss Pim observed dryly that she was rather thin—but then every one had said that—and Stacy answered cheerfully that that was a good thing. She had just made an interesting discovery. ... She had imagined Miss Pim's eyes to be like the eyes of Miss Postgate, and they were not in the least. Miss Postgate's eyes never smiled even when her lips did. Miss Pim's smile began at her eyes and spread to the rest of her face.

There was the Needlework Show to be examined by old students, who all showered it with superior praises, thinking in their secret hearts that it was a poor thing compared with the efforts of their own last term. There was a hilarious luncheon in the great hall, and the Principal's garden party in the afternoon, and in the evening a most amusing play by present students, full of topical allusions that constantly brought down the house, though to outsiders they would have been completely meaningless. And Stacy had been so long accustomed to feeling herself the most shabbily dressed person in any assembly that she no longer thought about it, or allowed it to spoil her pleasure in the least.

Sunday began with the sober beauty of a corporate Communion in the familiar great old church, which (a point thoroughly appreciated by Stacy after a solid month of St. Philibert's) had never known incense since the days of the Reformation. And then the hours began to fly with an unexampled speed in all sorts of delightful ways; and the immense afternoon picnic was entirely successful, and practically free from wasps; and then—well, then Stacy was in the train again and it was all over. She would have loved to stay for the Principal's usual Sunday evening reception; but she had promised faithfully to be back at ten, so that was out of the question. And she kept her word with the most literal exactness, ringing the front door bell of Number Seventeen as St. Philibert's clock began to strike. It was raining in Upper Galling, a dismal, dirty suburban drizzle. Also, it struck Stacy for the first time, as she stood waiting to be let in, that she was extremely tired.

Something else struck her after a minute: there was no light in the drawing-room window, which was most unusual on a Sunday evening. Also, it was most unusual that she was not let in at once. Miss Postgate would not, of course, hear of such a thing as a latch-key, but she was punctilious in being at hand to open the door as soon as she heard the bell. Stacy rang again, a little louder, and still nothing happened. She looked in alarm at her watch: surely she couldn't have mistaken the hour and returned at eleven? But no, all was well; besides, she had counted the strokes of St. Philibert's as she waited.

She stood back and looked up, and there was no light in Miss Postgate's bedroom window above the drawing-room. It was the most incomprehensible thing in the world. Neither

Miss Willie nor Miss Georgie ever went out in the evening except on Sundays, when they took it in turns to go to church; and in any case it was a rule of the Medes and Persians that the house must never be left empty. Stacy rang a third time, and again nothing happened.

She turned first hot and then cold with a sudden horrible idea. Was Miss Postgate so much annoyed with her for going away that she had locked her out on purpose? But the whole business had been thoroughly thrashed out, and there was no doubt that Stacy had paid handsomely beforehand for her short leave. Besides, Miss Postgate, though chilly and what Stacy called "mingy," had always proved herself a just mistress, never spiteful or liable to fits of temper; so it couldn't be that. If she were, for any incomprehensible reason, locked out, what on earth was she to do? Except Mrs. Blott, she knew no one in the place; and she didn't at all fancy spending the night in Mrs. Blott's one room. Also, it was beginning to rain quite hard. She put out her hand and tried the door-handle, and, to her extreme astonishment, it turned.

She stepped quickly inside out of the rain into a dark and silent house, and stood for a minute in the narrow little hall trying to make up her mind what to do. If her mistresses had gone to bed early—most unlikely, for their unbroken habit was to retire (Miss Postgate's word) at exactly half-past ten—they would much dislike being disturbed in their rooms now. If they were ill, they would surely have left some sort of note for her to find on her return; and they would have done the same if for some inexplicable reason they were out. Stacy had a little flash-lamp in her bag, and she switched it on and looked about expectantly. There was nothing—no note, no sound, no light.

She was dead tired; and, whatever else was or was not expected of her, she was supposed to go to bed at ten. She waited for another minute, trying to decide whether she ought or ought not to fasten the front door, and finally left it as it was. If her ladies had been called out in a hurry, which seemed the most unlikely thing in the world, they might have forgotten their latch-keys; and Stacy could not hear the doorbell up in her attic room. She thought of Miss Postgate, locked out on her own doorstep in a steady drenching rain, and went upstairs. She was probably doing the wrong thing, but it really wasn't her fault. She fell into bed after the rapidest possible preparation and slept without moving until …

She stirred drowsily, opened sleepy eyes, noticed something unusual in the sunlight on the wall, looked at her watch, and flew out of bed in horror. She had forgotten to wind her alarum clock! St. Philibert's, in a most accusing voice, was striking—nine.

Perhaps no cook ever dressed more quickly, or slipped downstairs more noiselessly, or felt more like a schoolgirl about to face a justly incensed head mistress. By this time hot water should have been taken to the bedrooms, and breakfast been cooked and served and cleared, ready for Mrs. Blott to wash up when she came at half-past nine. Stacy should have had her own breakfast long ago, and her kitchen and larder should now be in process of meticulous tidying before Miss Postgate came down to give the day's orders at ten. And there was no gas-ring; and the range was an old-fashioned *beast*—it would not supply any hot water for half an hour to come, let alone breakfast. … Stacy more than half expected to be summoned into Miss Postgate's bedroom as she passed for summary execution. But no, not a sound. It was, perhaps, more characteristic that Miss Postgate should wait in awful wrath for the usual ceremonies to be performed, and *then* come down on the defaulter with all the terrors of the law.

Under such circumstances it is, of course, well known that any kitchen fire will show the very worst side of its character; and the Postgate range was, as has been said, a plain beast.

Stacy raked and lit, and re-raked and re-lit, and blew with the bellows, and coaxed with a sheet of newspaper, which of course caught fire and flared out at her and scorched her hands. But at least the fire was burning by that time; and the kettle boiled at long last, and Stacy went trembling upstairs with her two cans of hot water.

It was perhaps cowardly, but it was certainly wise to call Miss Georgie first. She was not likely to be angry, for she dearly loved to lie in bed; and she would explain the mystery of last night and give Stacy some inkling as to the present lie

Stacy knocked.

of the land. Stacy knocked, perhaps a little faintly, received no answer, knocked again, still receiving no answer, opened the door and went in. It was not the first time that she had found Miss Georgie sound asleep, though surely it was odd that she should sleep as late as this.

She paused upon the threshold with a sudden feeling that things were all wrong.

The blind was up; and that was most unusual, for Miss Georgie's eyes were a little weak and she liked her bedroom well darkened. The window was of course shut, for the Misses Postgate belonged to the generation that mistrusted night air, even in summer. But that was always the case, and it was not usual to find this ... this ... Well, the room was horrible, as if it had not been aired for days-and worse than that. Miss Georgie's clothes, usually laid tidily on a chair as, presumably, she had learned to lay them in childhood, were on the floor, all anyhow. Miss Georgie herself was huddled up in bed, with the clothes pulled up round her in any sort of disorder and her face turned away.

"Miss Georgie! I'm afraid I'm very late this morning," said Stacy; and even to herself her voice sounded faint and frightened. But it was not half so odd as Miss Georgie's answering voice.

"Is ... that ... you ... at ... last ... Anastasia?"

Stacy put down her can in a hurry and ran forward.

"Yes," she said. "Oh, what is the matter? Are you ill?"

"Dying, I ... think," said Miss Georgie in the same unnatural voice.

As she made no movement Stacy went quickly round the bed to look at her, and was most thoroughly shocked and frightened by what she saw. How was it possible for such a change to take place in forty-eight hours? The round plump face had sagged and fallen in; and it was no longer pink, but of a horrid waxen colour. The greyish-fair hair, always primly plaited at night, was in a tousled mop. Her hand, when Stacy touched it, was cold and damp.

"Oh, Miss Georgie, can't you tell me what has happened?"

But Miss Georgie was past telling anything of the sort. She only murmured out a vague inquiry, almost too faint to catch, as to what day it was.

"Monday morning," Stacy told her, trembling, and that seemed to rouse her a little.

"Then you've only been ... away ... two days?"

"Not so long. I came back last night."

The heavy dark-circled eyes closed again, as if too weary to take that in. Miss Georgie gave a little quiver and lay still.

Stacy stepped quickly out of that room to the one next door. How odd that Miss Postgate should have left her sister alone when she was so ill! She only waited to knock once this time, opening the door almost immediately, and then stood quite still. But not so still as the figure lying on the bed.

The blind here was decently drawn down; but the sun was shining straight through it now, and everything was plainly visible in a yellowish light. The room was perfectly neat: Miss Postgate's clothes tidily folded on a chair, her hair neatly arranged in two short thin plaits, the bedclothes drawn up in precise folds. But Stacy knew, without going any nearer, that she was dead.

She slipped out of that second ghastly room and downstairs; and the uppermost thought in her mind was: Oh, if only she had never gone away!

There was, of course, no telephone in the house: Miss Postgate had always disapproved of these modern innovations. She could not leave Miss Georgie. She must call a neighbour ...

As she opened the front door (there were letters lying on the mat addressed to the two poor ladies upstairs: it was ghastly) she saw a small figure standing patiently at the foot of the steps looking as if it had stood there for some time. It was

Billy Blott. At sight of her he began to speak fast, as if reciting a well-known lesson.

"Please, Miss Cook, Mum's legs is bad. She's sorry she couldn't come yestiddy, nor yet she can't to-day. I did come yestiddy morning *an'* the day before, but I couldn't make no one hear."

"The ladies are—ill, Billy," said Stacy with a little gasp. "Can you go and fetch a doctor?"

"I ain't to cross no roads without Mum or you, never."

"No. But there is a doctor, I know, just round the corner on this side. Please go there as fast as you can, and ask him to come *now*."

"Right, Miss Cook!"

Billy humped himself away on his crutch and Stacy went indoors again. She was glad not to have summoned neighbours whom she didn't know, who would, she felt, run in and out, and fuss, and be horrible. She went up again to Miss Georgie, found her lying still with closed eyes, went vaguely down to the kitchen and made up her fire mechanically, went up again to the hall to wait. When Billy reappeared she beckoned him up the steps.

"I'm to come *in*, Miss Cook?" he inquired unbelievingly, and then began to pull himself up with alacrity, staring round the unfamiliar hall with sharp bright eyes. "Doctor's just been called out. They'll send him the minute he comes back."

"Oh!" said Stacy hopelessly; and then, quickly: "Billy, please stay till he comes."

She could not bear to be alone in the house, knowing what she knew.

"Right, Miss Cook!" said Billy, full of pride and importance.

"Your mother won't be frightened, will she?"

Billy screwed up his queer unchildlike little face.

"If she *is*," he said, "hearing about all this here will make up for it!"

"I … I'll get you something to eat," said Stacy. "Wait here. You'll never manage the kitchen stairs."

She ran down them with the speedy accuracy of long practice, opened the larder door, stood staring, with her hand at her throat. The place had been shut up, of course, for a great many hours, and the window was small. But that wouldn't account …

In any case, she couldn't investigate now, though it did occur to her that that leg of lamb, cooked on Friday, had seemed doubtful at the time—and this was Monday. But she had promised food of some sort to Billy; and the doctor might come at any moment; and Miss Georgie might be wanting her … She found bread, and a little treacle, and a very little tea; and the milkman had been, leaving the usual small bottle. It took her a minute or two to prepare even this very modest meal, for the hateful range had seized its chance to let the fire go dull, so that there was no boiling water. Then, with a little tray, she mounted again.

"Here, Billy!"

How very odd the child looked! Whiter even than usual, and bigger-eyed, and gazing at her in a strange, furtive fashion. Had he got into some mischief while she had been away?— stolen something even? For a moment Stacy's heart failed her, since she had broken that law of the Medes and Persians and invited him to come in; but the next moment she was ashamed of herself as the little hoarse voice piped out:

"Miss Cook, the lydy upstairs was calling for you!"

"Eat your breakfast, Billy," said Stacy, and ran upstairs full of self-reproach. No wonder the child was frightened if Miss Georgie had recovered enough to show that ghastly face on the landing above. …

But she had not.

"Miss Georgie, did you call me?" Stacy asked, trembling, from the doorway. But there was no answer. Going a little way into the room, she saw plainly enough that there never would be any answer.

It seemed years before the doctor came, running sharply up the front steps with his little bag, and asking intelligent questions in a hurry. He proved, to Stacy's relief (for she had sent Billy out at random, not knowing any local doctor), to be the one who had always attended her ladies. He made very little comment. He ran upstairs two steps at a time and was not gone very long.

"You realized, I suppose, that I had been called in too late?"

"The lydy upstairs was calling for you!"

Stacy nodded, for words were not convenient. She had sent
Billy home. She was sitting on the one hall chair listening to
the dreadful silence of the house. She followed the doctor
into the dining-room and listened to all he had to say, which
was not much. He had little doubt that her ladies had died of
ptomaine poisoning, but there must, of course, be an inquest.
Had she any idea what they had eaten during her absence?

It seemed so many years since that last Friday that Stacy had
to rack her brains for a moment before she remembered. She
had a vague recollection of the doubtful leg of lamb, but the
doctor shook his head over that suggestion. Since she was sure
of its having been well cooked, that ought not to have worked
such sudden havoc, even in the present heat. He would like to
look at the contents of the larder. ... Like Stacy, he halted on
the doorstep.

"Is that the mutton? It must be buried at once. ... Ha,
what's this?"

It was not entirely, or principally, the leg of lamb that was
making the larder so terrible. It was something, two somethings,
set out neatly on a plate under a wire cover.

"Sausages! In this weather!" said the doctor sharply. And
then, more sharply still, "Where did they come from?"

Stacy told him.

"Did Miss Postgate always deal at that little shop?"

Stacy said "Yes." She had always privately thought it a
horrible dirty little shop; she had always had a conviction that
Miss Postgate dealt there because it was cheap. She saw, in the
doctor's eye, that his opinion on both points was the same as
her own. He repeated firmly that the lamb should be buried at
once, but he took away with him the two revolting sausages,
well interred in layers of grease-proof paper, with thick brown
paper over that.

CHAPTER XII

A Newspaper Placard

LIKE most of us, Stacy loved detective-stories: like most of us, she read constantly of inquests: like most of us, she never imagined the possibility that she herself might have to appear at one, still less that she would be the most important witness—the only one, in fact, who could give any evidence at all, when the doctor had had his say. How and what she had cooked for the final meals, before she started on that fatal holiday, the reason why she had left her own share untasted, the illness of Mrs. Blott, which had prevented her from doing her usual work at Number Seventeen on those days of all others. There had been no end to the questions asked; there had been a few awful moments when she herself had seemed to be suspected of wilfully doing away with her employers, but that had not lasted long. The doctor had spoken up pretty sharply, giving evidence of other occasions when he had been called in for minor illnesses, due to Miss Postgate's passion for cheap and nasty food, and his repeated and unheeded warnings to her. The coroner also was a merciful man, obviously sorry for the white-faced girl who had returned to meet such an appalling shock; and he pointed out with no uncertain voice that, if the fault had in any way been Stacy's, she would certainly not have left the fatal sausages lying in the larder when she went away. But he dealt pretty severely after that with the butcher who kept the dirty little shop where those sausages were bought. And Stacy listened to it all dully, and then all was over and she was free to go—where?

Number Seventeen was closed. Nevertheless, crowds of people had made pilgrimages to it, staring and gaping and wondering, and saying, There! They had always *said* No Sausages in the Summer, and don't you forget it in future, Maria Jane! The doctor's wife had most kindly taken Stacy in for the time, and had been everything that was good and helpful; but naturally she couldn't stay there when everything was over. They went together to the funeral, a pitiful affair, attended only by themselves, and Mrs. Blott and Billy, and one or two neighbouring friends, and three men. One of these, a most unattractive person who looked at every one with suspicion, was reputed to be a distant Postgate relation whom the poor ladies had particularly disliked. One was an elderly man whom Stacy had never seen before. The third, with him, was the Mr. Harbinger who had called to see Miss Georgie two or three hundred years ago.

The doctor's wife, who was little and brisk and tactful, parted from Stacy at the cemetery gates—she must rush home to her baby! And Stacy was thankful to turn back and cry a little in peace among the gravestones, with no one to see or care. Her outlook really was extremely dismal. She had not only lost her job, but, far more serious, she had lost her reference; and it sounds bad for an out-of-work cook to confess that her last mistress died of ptomaine poisoning. But she would *not* go back to Mr. and Mrs. Phipps. That was quite certain.

She dried her eyes at last and walked slowly back to the doctor's house. The streets were full of people hurrying to their dinners or their luncheons, as the case might be; and paperboys were yelling the contents of those absurd evening papers that are on sale about the middle of the day. "Horful Tragedy," Stacy heard, and "Shocking Suicide," and "Death of a …" she couldn't hear what. It seemed as if the whole world was miserable. Stacy wondered, vaguely, why papers couldn't sometimes bill a few cheerful events for a change.

"That's right!" said the doctor's little wife, brisk and kind, waiting at her front door for Stacy. "Just in time for lunch. Hugh won't be in, *as* usual! Don't you ever marry a doctor, Stacy, if you want any peace in life. The bell will ring by the time you've washed your hands."

It was her face that Stacy wanted to wash, but that was tactfully left unmentioned. She was half-way upstairs when she was called back.

"Wait a minute! Here's a letter for you that came while we were out."

It had been re-directed by the post office; and it was the one thing calculated to hearten Stacy—a letter from Agatha, who, of course, knew nothing of these last tragic days. Stacy always wrote to her on Sundays; and she had written in the train, on the way back from her Guild meeting, and had posted the letter before she crossed London, and had never had the heart to write since. It would be wonderful to hear news from some one who was happy, to be reminded that there still was some happiness left in the world. …

Stacy stood with the envelope in one hand and its contents in the other. There was no letter at all, for you really couldn't dignify by that name the torn scrap of paper with half a dozen words on it—so absolutely unlike Agatha, who wrote the prettiest neat hand that never varied, and was extremely particular about her note paper.

"Please, *please*, Stacy, come at once!"

That was all—in writing, at least. Folded carelessly and unevenly into the envelope (again so unlike Agatha's tidy ways) were four one-pound notes. And that was the only thing that was like Agatha, who, whatever her own trouble, had remembered, in spite of it, that Stacy might not have enough money for another journey.

The luncheon bell rang. Stacy flew downstairs just as she was—she had never even reached her room. She showed her letter. She must go; must go at once! Agatha was her dearest friend. …

Little Mrs. Lucas, kind as ever but extremely business-like, had the whole thing out of her in a twinkling: Agatha's name, where she lived, how long it took to get there. Within two minutes she had hunted up all necessary details of trains and the whole journey was neatly planned. There was a train from Euston at three, and it was now just after one. There was plenty of time for Stacy to eat, pack, and rest a little; and all these things must and should be done.

"What's the good of your dashing off now and spending an hour by yourself at Euston? for *I'm* not coming with you till I've had my own lunch and given the children their dinner!" said Mrs. Lucas, carving mutton briskly. "*Sit down*, Stacy! If you don't, I'll ring up Hugh—I know where he is—and he'll come and stop you from going at all!"

So, since obedience was the easiest plan, Stacy obeyed, choked down a certain amount of food without in the least knowing its kind or taste, had her suit-case packed for her with great skill and quickness, and was finally escorted with the utmost kindness across London and into her proper train exactly five minutes before it was due to start.

"I've ordered a tea-basket for you; and mind you eat every scrap of food in it," said Mrs. Lucas authoritatively. "You don't know what you're going into, and quite likely you'll get no regular meal to-night; and there's no use in arriving a perfect wreck and being useless. *Do* you know where your ticket is? *Is* your purse safe? Here's a paper and a shilling shocker; and do let me have just a line tomorrow, my dear girl, for we shan't be happy about you till we know something."

Performing her very last kindness, she left immediately, before the train started, and Stacy was free to sit back in her corner seat and do nothing. Perhaps in a little while her head would stop going round and round and she would be able to think clearly again. Though thinking was of no use whatever, since she had nothing to go upon in her bewilderment. Perhaps … perhaps …

It was the tea-basket (paid for, as she subsequently discovered) which roused her from a most comforting sleep; and by that time she was well upon her way. She roused herself with some little difficulty, but found, when the first shaky cup had been poured out, that she was amazingly refreshed and able to face things steadily. It was, of course, useless to sit and wonder and worry; she would know soon enough what had really happened. She opened her newspaper. …

It struck her in large letters on the front page.

"SUICIDE OF WELL-KNOWN BARONET. FAMOUS
EXPLORER DIES AT HOME.
PORTRAIT OF …"

No need for Stacy to read the caption under that. She had seen, often enough, those alert bright eyes smiling at her. She had listened, entirely agreeing, to Agatha's gentle raptures over her father's perfections of form and face and character. And now here was the account of Sir Humphrey Phayre's being discovered dead in his dressing-room—not, oh, *not* by Agatha?

No. Mercifully, it had been the chauffeur who had found him, and had had sense enough to lock the door before any one else could see what he had seen. No one had heard the shot, or at least taken any notice of it. Corn was being cut close by, and rabbit-shooting was in full swing. "Miss Phayre was totally prostrated. …"

The miles sped by after that unnoticed by Stacy, except that it seemed she would never arrive, never reach Agatha to help and comfort her. She had a vague idea, afterwards, that one or two of her fellow-passengers had stared at her, and asked if anything was the matter, and that she hadn't answered

In large letters on the front page.

them at all. At long, long last the Welsh hills began to rise all around her; and then she suddenly began to dread the moment of arrival, and to hope wildly that each little country station would not be the right one. But at last, inevitably, the well-known name showed up on its little painted board; and Stacy stepped out, feeling cold and looking pale. ... What a different arrival from the last, when Agatha had been smiling there to meet her!

Since Mrs. Lucas, in thinking of everything, had remembered to send a telegram giving the time of her arrival,

the car was there to meet her, and the chauffeur was taking
her case and touching his cap. She hadn't liked him very much,
she remembered, during her former visit; she had thought his
manner brusque and disagreeable, and had secretly wondered
why Sir Humphrey had engaged him. It was even more
definitely brusque and disagreeable now; but what wonder,
seeing how the worst of the shock had fallen on him! Stacy
faltered out an inquiry about Agatha. But he knew nothing; he
hadn't seen her. And so they rolled, in silence, up and down
the steep narrow roads, and Stacy dreaded the moment of
arrival more and more. But it came at last, as everything does,
and the sight of all blinds drawn down where she had spent
such a gay and light-hearted week was like a blow. Somehow,
she had never thought of that.

Miss Phayre was in her room. She had asked that Miss
Wayland should go straight up to her. …

"I remember the way; don't come!" said Stacy hastily, and
ran upstairs.

She couldn't have borne, in any case, the formality of
being shown stiffly up and announced; but the maid, like the
chauffeur, looked—odd. It wasn't that she had been crying, or
anything like that; quite definitely, she had not. But there was
something about her look and her manner for which Stacy
could find no words: a sullenness, a resentment, a suppressed
sense of injury. Of course, this was a terrible happening,
and, of course, all the servants were of only a couple of
months' service, with no long-standing personal interest in
their employers; and, of course, every one said that servants
nowadays think only of themselves. …

All this ran rapidly through Stacy's head, almost without her
knowing it, as she mounted the stairs. Perhaps, now that the
meeting with Agatha was so near, she was afraid to think of
it, and would rather turn her thoughts in any other direction.
She knocked softly at the door, heard a very faint answer from

within, went in, to see a forlorn figure sitting desolate by the darkened window. ...

"Oh, Stacy! Oh, Stacy!" a voice, faintly like Agatha's, wailed to her. "Oh, I have wanted you so—and they won't even let me see him!"

CHAPTER XIII

Unopened Envelopes

WHEN, a long time after, Stacy went downstairs a tall thin figure, restlessly roaming about the hall, turned to meet her. It was Mr. Blount.

"How is she?" he asked hoarsely without any form of greeting.

"She's quite quiet now, and I have made her have something to eat. I think she will go to sleep," said Stacy in a voice that shook. She walked into the drawing-room, and he followed her: such a charming room two months ago, and now inexplicably desolate. It looked as if it had not been dusted, and withered flowers hung in the vases. Sir Humphrey's pipe lay on a little table near Agatha's work-basket, and its ashes were still in an ash-tray near.

"Can I do anything?" Mr. Blount asked abruptly.

"I don't know. I only came this evening. … Have you seen her?"

"No. What right have I to worry her? She must know that I—I'd do anything in the world for her."

"Have you told her so?" Stacy asked him point-blank.

He laughed, not a merry laugh.

"What right have I to tell her anything of the sort? What have I got to offer her? I have three hundred a year and my vicarage; you've seen what that is like. Compare it with this!"

He looked round the darkening room; and certainly, even in its present neglected condition, it was very different from that great empty barrack of his. But Stacy persisted.

"She will have plenty of money."

"And that is exactly why I can't ask her!"

"But she has a *right* to know."

"I have no right to tell her. I can't ask her to marry me; and she would be sorry for me; and I wouldn't hurt her for the world."

He went and stared haggardly at a smiling portrait of Agatha hanging on the wall.

"Well, I can't do anything to-night, I suppose," he said abruptly. "I'll be down here first thing in the morning; and—you'll let me help in any way I can?"

"I shall be only too thankful," Stacy assured him honestly. Indeed, she felt utterly at a loss, with a second inquest and a second funeral hanging over her, and Agatha to be shielded as much as was humanly possible from all the attendant horrors. Besides, though it was a very minor worry, there was something unnatural about the house. She had had to ring Agatha's bell three times before any answer came; and during her late visit a mere touch had been enough from any room. Her request for sandwiches and hot coffee, and anything else that was sustaining and could be taken with little trouble, had been received sulkily and unwillingly. It had been a long time before a tray arrived; and then its burden was such as Stacy could not have imagined in that house—half-cold coffee of a greyish colour, ill-cut lumpy sandwiches, nothing else at all. Fortunately, Agatha was far too much exhausted to notice any of these things. She submissively ate and drank a certain amount, and then allowed Stacy to help her into bed, and lay still.

Stacy rang again, from the drawing-room, and again had to repeat her ring, and to wait.

"Am I to sleep in the same room that I had when I was here before?"

She was told sullenly that the maid didn't know; no orders had been given.

"Do you mean that no room is ready for me?"

Apparently that was the case. No orders had been given.

Stacy was tired to death, and thoroughly out of heart; also, though she had eaten one or two of Agatha's sandwiches to encourage her to do the same, she was extremely hungry. But she had not been trained under Miss Pim for nothing; and she was not red-haired for nothing either. She forgot her weariness. She spoke in a sharp voice, with authority.

"Kindly ask Mrs. Sargent to come and speak to me here, at once."

It was several minutes before the housekeeper put in an appearance, and during those minutes Stacy's wrath kindled. At the first sight of that resentful countenance she girded up her loins for battle.

"Good-evening, Mrs. Sargent."

"Good-evening!"

"This is all very terrible."

"Very."

"You probably know that Miss Phayre telegraphed for me to come to her?"

A stony stare was the only answer. Stacy had never liked the looks of Mrs. Sargent, though on her first visit she had had almost nothing to do with her, and she thought now that she had never seen a more unpleasant expression.

"I said," she repeated, slowly and distinctly, "that Miss Phayre telegraphed for me to come and help her; and I came at once. She is quite unfit to do anything at all, and she has begged me to attend to everything for her. You will therefore take your orders from me."

"I shall do *what*?"

Mrs. Sargent was a great deal bigger than Stacy, being a bulky woman of middle age, and she seemed now to swell with anger. But Stacy's blood was up.

"I said," she repeated, again slowly and distinctly, "that

you—will—take—your—orders—from—me. Do you understand that?"

Mrs. Sargent merely glared. But Stacy, quite unafraid, glared back. She had forgotten that she was tired and hungry. Like all red-haired people, she loved a fight.

"I had to ring three times from Miss Phayre's bedroom before any one came. I ordered food for her; it came after a good deal of delay, and it was hardly eatable when it came. I am surprised that you allow the under-servants to behave like that when there is trouble in the house."

She had thrown down the gage of battle with a vengeance now, and she knew it, for she had implied, with intention, that the great Mrs. Sargent was only herself a servant, like the rest of her staff. She waited, unafraid, for the disagreeable answer that was sure to come. It came with a rush.

"You seem to take a good deal upon yourself, Miss What's-your-name ..."

"My name is Miss Wayland, and you know it perfectly well," Stacy broke clearly into the storm. "Yes. I *am* taking a good deal upon myself, since there is no one else at present to do it. If you had behaved as I am sure Miss Phayre expected, I should have had no occasion to say all this. Now, please take my orders."

She paused to allow of any answer, but there was none. Mrs. Sargent gasped for breath, looking furious; but her eyes fell, and she seemed to have shrunk a little.

"I have had a long journey, and I am extremely tired," Stacy told her. "Please send me a tray of food—*eatable* food—here as quickly as possible. After that I shall expect to find my room ready for me, the same room that I had when I was here before. I will see you again in the morning. Good-night."

Answer came there none. Mrs. Sargent had met her match, and she knew it; but she was not going to acknowledge defeat with a good grace. She stalked silently out of the room, and in a remarkably short space of time there arrived the sort of picnic meal that might have been expected in that house— chicken and salad, and jelly, and wine, and cake, all perfectly served. Stacy ate and drank with a good appetite; and went up, twenty minutes later, to find her room in apple-pie order, even to an entirely unnecessary hot-water bottle; and slept like the Seven Sleepers; and woke refreshed to find early tea awaiting her, with a mild if sullen inquiry as to what time she would like breakfast. And so on, and so on—her victory seemed complete.

Agatha proved, mercifully, to be only too thankful to stay in bed in her darkened room. So Stacy went down, and had hardly finished an excellent and well-served breakfast before Mr. Blount was upon her, begging to be allowed to make all necessary business arrangements, to which Stacy most willingly consented. He also brought a letter from that kind and chatty Lady Marjorie Cray, who had first brought him to Sir Humphrey's house. She was in Scotland, was most distressed to hear the terrible news, would come and see Agatha, and do anything she could to help, the moment she reached home again. It seemed to Stacy that the worst of the storm was over—if only Agatha would be willing to stay in her room until after the funeral. And Agatha, mercifully, was willing. She was completely crushed. She was meekly acquiescent in any plans that were made for her good. The blinds were up again, and the house looking itself, before she came down, very pale, in her pathetic black frock, good and sweet and grateful, relying on Stacy and Mr. Blount for everything.

"Stacy, what should I have done without you!"

Stacy, privately, didn't know; also, she had a fresh private discomfort which she hoped but didn't expect to keep from Agatha. Once more there was that nameless something wrong about the house, and several times she had had to speak pretty sharply about slovenlinesses and neglects which she could not allow to pass. While Agatha was invisible upstairs in her bed the servants had reluctantly accepted Stacy as her understudy. Now that she was down again, that could no longer continue. … Even as she brooded over this disagreeable prospect a message was brought, inquiring if Mrs. Sargent could speak to Miss Phayre.

"But of course!" said Agatha, gentle and courteous. "I shall be very glad to see her."

Stacy withdrew into a remote chair. There would probably be all sorts of accusations against herself, which would be unpleasant; but she didn't really care two pins. Her conscience was quite clear, and she knew that she had done for Agatha what Agatha could never have done for herself.

"Good-morning, Mrs. Sargent," the kind and gentle voice was saying.

"Good-morning!" replied exactly the same voice that had greeted Stacy on her arrival; so much so that it surprised even Agatha. She looked up with a mild inquiry at the flushed and sullen face confronting her.

"I hope you are better, Miss Phayre."

"Yes, thank you," Agatha answered. "Miss Wayland has taken such care of me; and I am afraid I have been …"

Mrs. Sargent, not at all interested in her remarks, cut into them.

"I wish to leave immediately."

"To leave?" Agatha repeated, bewildered. "*Now?*"

"Immediately!" Mrs. Sargent repeated, more truculent than before. "I should like to be paid my salary and go to-day."

Agatha was always gentle, but she could be dignified on occasion. She rose now and stood confronting her house-keeper.

"Certainly, Mrs. Sargent. If you do not wish to stay, I should be very sorry to keep you. Do you give me any reason?"

Mrs. Sargent stared at her, half-spoke, and then thinking

"I should like to go to-day."

better of it, jerked out brusquely, "I prefer not to give my reasons!"

"Very well, then," said Agatha. "I will write your cheque at once."

She turned away to do so, but was stopped.

"One moment, Miss Phayre! To save you trouble, I may as well tell you that the whole of your staff wishes to leave."

Agatha, cheque-book in hand, turned and stared at her.

"I do not understand."

"Perhaps not! I think you soon will."

Stacy could bear this no longer. She rose and came forward.

"This is all most unfit for Miss Phayre," she said icily. "I am sure she accepts the resignations of *all* of you. Please go away. You will be paid as soon as possible."

Mrs. Sargent glared at her furiously; but she remembered their earlier battle, and was too clever to offer herself again for defeat. As on that earlier occasion, she stalked out without a word.

"Oh, Stacy, what does all this mean?" Agatha asked pitifully.

"I don't know," was Stacy's grim answer. "But I do know that you are well quit of every one of them!"

"But what shall we *do*?"

"We shall do perfectly well. Pay them off, and let them go."

"I don't think I have enough money," said Agatha, looking a little frightened. "Father always paid my allowance into the bank; but I have bought a good many things this quarter, and I don't know how much anybody is paid. *He* always did that sort of thing."

"You have his keys, haven't you?"

"Yes. They were brought up to me. ..."

Agatha turned white, and trembled. The question brought back to her, only too vividly, the terrible news that had been brought up to her with the keys.

"Let us ask Mr. Blount," said Stacy sensibly.

Mr. Blount, needless to say, was close at hand, and only too anxious to be of use, well-informed also, and explaining gently to Agatha that she could not use any of her father's money until his will had been proved. But he himself would go over at once to the county town, where Sir Humphrey had banked, and come to some arrangement with the manager. It was always done, he believed, in such circumstances; he was quite sure that there would be no difficulty at all, and that Agatha had no occasion for worry. So he went. And Stacy, who felt oddly uneasy and dissatisfied, persuaded Agatha to go upstairs again to her room, out of the way of any possible further annoyance.

She herself came down again and sat waiting. It seemed a very long time. She thought and thought, and could come to no conclusion at all; only she felt, more and more strongly, that something unknown was very wrong. When she saw Mr. Blount's face, on his return, she was quite sure of it.

"Well?" she said, getting up to meet him.

"Where is she?" he returned, looking anxiously round. "You are sure she won't come down?"

Stacy was quite sure. She listened in silence to his incredible, annihilating news.

The bank manager had received him coldly. It was true Sir Humphrey had always banked there ever since he came into Wales; but there was now no money of his in the bank at all. In fact, his account was overdrawn to quite a large extent. Under the circumstances the manager did not feel justified in advancing any money to Miss Phayre, though he quite appreciated that she was in a very difficult position. ... Mr. Blount's remarks about him were quite unfit for clerical use, but he certainly had reason to feel strongly.

"What is to be done?" he ended, staring at Stacy. "She seems to have no relations or old friends ..."

"She left me his keys," Stacy suggested. And Mr. Blount reprehensibly remarked that he didn't care two straws about the law, and they would just see what money they could find ...

This was an easy task, for they found none. Instead, they found piles and piles and piles of unopened envelopes such as Stacy, during her last visit, had seen Sir Humphrey throwing impatiently into the waste-paper basket—and every one of them contained an unpaid bill. Bills of all sorts and kinds, large and small, from local creditors and London creditors, and even farther afield: ordinary polite bills, others with a covering note saying that an early settlement would oblige, others again threatening "legal proceedings." Stacy and Mr. Blount paused very soon in their search and stared at each other, aghast.

"What is to be done?" they asked in the same breath. And Stacy added incredulously, "But he was so *rich*! There must be some mistake; he must just have put off paying!"

Mr. Blount had found an account-book, and was studying it with a puzzled frown. Up to a certain date, not so very long ago, Sir Humphrey seemed to have paid all his debts like any one else, then, quite suddenly, he had ceased to make any such payments at all. Among these entries were the wages of all his servants—very large wages, ranging from Mrs. Sargent's hundred-and-fifty a year downwards. It appeared pretty certain that all these were owing for the last two months. No wonder that the household had been unlike itself! Not much wonder that they had now risen in a body and given notice.

"How much does it come to?" Stacy asked in a low and alarmed tone, looking over his shoulder. He finished the calculation, and they looked at each other again with horror.

"What *shall* we do?" Stacy gasped, taking it for granted, as a matter of course, that they were working together to shelter Agatha.

"Have you any money? Can you get any?" he inquired without apology. But Stacy shook her head in despair. She had a couple of pounds or so; what remained from the notes that Agatha had sent her. There was no one in the world whom she could ask for more.

Mr. Blount did not trouble to state his own want of cash; he had never made any secret of it. He sat staring straight before him, with his head down and his clasped hands hanging between his knees.

"Agatha has a good deal of jewellery ..." Stacy suggested tentatively.

"The money is wanted *now*. There would be no time to sell anything. And besides …"

He did not finish the sentence; and there was no need, for Stacy knew exactly what he meant. They were trying to save Agatha from the knowledge of this dreadful state of things. Beyond that, in both their minds was a horrid doubt that that jewellery, like so much else, was unpaid for.

He stood up suddenly, with the expression of a man who has made a most distasteful resolution.

"If Lady Marjorie were at home I am sure she would come to the rescue. I can telegraph to her …"

"But …" said Stacy, and found that she was speaking to empty air. He was the sort of man who, faced with a disagreeable task, gets through with it as soon as possible; he was already whirring down the drive on his ancient bicycle.

She locked all Sir Humphrey's tell-tale drawers again with exceeding care, and went up to return the keys to Agatha. In her room they would at least be safe. Anywhere downstairs, Stacy did not trust Mrs. Sargent and her underlings for a moment.

"Is everything settled? Have they gone?" Agatha asked, lifting a very sad face that was puzzled as well as distressed. No young mistress could ever have been more kind and considerate to her servants, and she was hurt beyond measure that they could have turned upon her now, at such a time, in such a manner.

"Not yet," said Stacy briefly, and said nothing more. She could not save Agatha from this disillusionment; she could hardly hope to shield her from the much worse one that concerned Sir Humphrey.

CHAPTER XIV

The Only Proper Ending

"IT'S all right," said Mr. Blount breathlessly to a white-faced Stacy who hardly dared ask questions. "Lady Marjorie has telegraphed enough money to tide us over. . . . She's a marvel."

"I didn't know you *could* telegraph money," said Stacy, relieved but incredulous.

"Oh, yes; no difficulty about that. Come along and let us get rid of these brutes as fast as possible."

He sat at the gate-legged table in the hall, very stern and contemptuous, and summoned the household to appear before him and receive what was due to them—yes, even Mrs. Sargent and the chauffeur had to come with the others and be paid in cash or go without. When the last young maid was paid off he stood up and dusted his hands with his handkerchief; a very old one, Stacy could not help observing, with a large hole in one corner.

"Now go, every one of you!" he said briefly. "And if you dare to ask Miss Phayre for references, *I* will write them for you."

They slunk away variously moved: Mrs. Sargent trying to maintain an empurpled dignity against great odds, the chauffeur scowling vindictively, one or two of the others making faint excuses.

"It's been very trying for *us* . . ."

"We can't afford to go long without our money . . ."

Roger Blount took no notice of them at all. He stalked through the house, ostentatiously locking the door of every room that contained anything of value. He went out and locked the garage. With his hands full of keys, he came back to Stacy in the hall, almost falling over a small scullery-maid on the way. She was dressed to leave, lugging a heavy suit-case, crying:

"Oh, please, miss, how is Miss Phayre?"

"Very unwell and unhappy," Stacy told her sternly.

The girl burst out sobbing.

"Oh, please, miss, I never wanted to do it! I don't *want* to leave Miss Phayre. She's been that good to me and my little sister what's blind. They *made* me ..."

Roger Blount gave her a pat on the shoulder.

"That's all right, child. I'm sure they made it hard for you to be brave; but we can't have any cowards here, and you can't stay. We want Miss Phayre to forget all about this as fast as possible—if she can."

The girl crept away sobbing; and shortly afterwards, the telephone having worked overtime in summoning taxis, the house was empty. Stacy and Roger looked at each other.

"That's a relief!" he said shortly.

"Yes, indeed!" said Stacy; but she realized, as he did not for a moment, the difficulties of the position in which Agatha was left.

"We can take a breathing space before we go on to find out what is left for her," said Roger; and his expression said a great deal more. Rich Agatha had been, in his eyes, entirely out of his reach, poor Agatha was a different matter altogether. ... As he spoke, she came very quietly downstairs.

"I saw them all go. ... They are *all* gone, aren't they?" she asked timidly.

"All gone!" Stacy assured her.

"But ... what are we going to do now?"

"*You* are going to sit in the garden and talk things over with Mr. Blount," said Stacy; and departed, chin in air, towards what house-agents alluringly call "the offices."

Well, she had expected pretty much what she found. It

is astonishing how quickly servants go to pieces and neglect their duties when the house is upset in any way; and in this case the underlings had been set the worst of examples. It seemed to the dismayed but unsurprised Stacy that hardly one thing was in its proper place: kitchen and larder in disorder, pantry stacked with unwashed silver, a miserable cat mewing by a saucer of sour milk. Stacy saw to that at once before she did anything else. Then she took a general survey, and decided that luncheon was obviously the next necessity. No lack of food here, at any rate! She ransacked the larder, chose what

"*I saw them all go.*"

seemed to her best, and was competently ringing the gong twenty minutes after.

"But, Stacy, I thought you said they had all gone?" said Agatha, wide-eyed, coming in from the garden.

"So they have."

"But …"

"Come and eat something, for goodness' sake!" Stacy bade her peremptorily. "I'm hungry, if you are not; and Mr. Blount must be starved. He's been rushing about all the morning."

It was easy to see that they had been very happy in the garden. A little colour had crept back into Agatha's white cheeks, and Roger Blount's eyes were shining; and both of them, although apparently in a sort of trance, ate quite respectably. After that they feebly attempted to help in clearing away and washing up, and it was a question which was the more incompetent.

"But, Stacy, how dreadful everything looks!" the dismayed Agatha commented, surveying the kitchen that she had never seen except in the pink of perfection.

"Foul!" Stacy agreed briefly.

It was indeed a sorry sight. Hardly anything was in its proper place; and nearly everything looked dirty.

"But what shall we *do*?"

Stacy looked at her critically. She could hardly imagine Agatha working with her hands, and she herself would gladly have scrubbed her fingers to the bone for her. But she was a girl of sense. She knew that nothing in the world is so noxious as idle brooding over troubles. Therefore:

"We must get it all straight again as fast as possible," was her entirely practical reply.

"*We?*" stammered the girl who had no practical knowledge whatever.

"Yes; you and I! You can't possibly ask new servants to come into a place looking like this," said the girl who had been trained, hiding in the most secret recesses of her heart her grave doubt whether Agatha would ever have any money to pay any servants.

"But I'm afraid …"

"Do you know how to clean silver?"

Agatha shook her head forlornly.

"Then you'd better learn," said Stacy briskly, hardening her heart. It had seemed to her, in a rapid survey of the work before them, that this was perhaps the job most suited to a person who had never had to do anything. She had never realized what a thankless and difficult task lay before herself.

It seemed incredible that Agatha, so clever at school, should prove so stupid over this, or that the long white fingers, so deft and quick at embroidery, should be so clumsy now. Stacy gave a brisk elementary lesson, and finally left her pupil to do her best—or worst, as seemed likely to be the case. She herself shut the kitchen door behind her and fell to work with a will.

"Stacy, is this right? … *Oh!*"

"Yes, I know I'm not fit to be seen," Stacy replied with a grin of amusement, answering the horrified tone of the last word. She got up, rather stiffly, from her knees and pushed her hair out of her eyes with the back of her hand. "I've been … rather busy."

"But … you've made the place look quite different already!"

"It needed to," Stacy returned briefly. "Wait a minute. I can't touch that till I've washed my hands."

"Is it right?" Agatha repeated wistfully.

Stacy took the sugar-sifter doubtfully offered her, which was far from "right"; and, having been brought up under Miss Pim's uncompromising rule, she said so, and said why.

"But, of course, you should have turned out the sugar first; it'll be full of dust and powder!"

"I never thought of that," Agatha confessed, abashed.

"And you haven't got the holes all clear; and you must brush with the *hard* brush till you get every scrap of black out of that groove; and, good gracious! you mustn't bring polished silver in your bare hands. Just look at your finger-marks all over it!"

Agatha looked frankly dismayed.

"Stacy, I *am* sorry. … But what an enormous amount there is to learn about even one thing like this!"

"One soon gets into the way of it," Stacy comforted her. "We had some pretty awful duds at College, and most of them turned out quite bright in the end. … What's that?"

"The postman."

"All right. I'll go!"

Before Agatha had time to realize that there was no one now to answer bells, Stacy had flashed out of the room. She had her own reasons—amply justified. She pushed away half a dozen ominous long envelopes to join their fellows in a drawer before returning to Agatha to report:

"Nothing for you. One for me."

"Oh, Stacy, is anything wrong?"

Agatha, watching Stacy's face as she read what seemed a very short letter, had grown alarmed. Poor thing, she had grown used to every fresh event proving a fresh unpleasantness.

"No, no!" Stacy hastened to reassure her. "I don't understand it; that's all."

She handed the short letter to Agatha, recalling quite suddenly a certain brass plate that she had passed dozens of times every time she turned out of St. Philibert's Terrace into Condover Road.

"Who is this writing?"

"He came once to see Miss Georgie, just before I went to the Guild meeting," said Stacy, realizing with a shock what a very little time ago that really was, though it felt like years. "I saw him at the funeral, too, with somebody older—the senior partner, I suppose."

"What very queer questions to ask!"

Stacy nodded.

"Mad," she said briefly. "But they won't take long to answer. I'd better get it done at once."

Still in a state of extreme dishevelment, she sat down at the great desk in the study—how full its drawers were of unpaid bills!—and composed a business-like answer.

> "DEAR MR. HARBINGER,—In answer to your questions: (1) Yes; the Misses Postgate were alone in the house when I returned to it. (2) Miss Wilhelmina was then already dead; Miss Georgiana died about half an hour later.
>
> "Yours truly,
>
> "A. WAYLAND."

"Where do I post this?" she inquired of Agatha, coming back with the envelope in her hand.

"Oh, put it in the box in the hall. Don't you remember? It is always cleared at six …"

Agatha stopped, staring at Stacy in fresh dismay.

"Well, it won't be cleared to-day," said Stacy a trifle grimly. "Where *is* the nearest box?"

Agatha blankly returned that she didn't know. The nearest post office was close to the station, five miles away. She had no idea where "they" had taken the letters when the hall-box was cleared every evening. …

It was merciful that Roger Blount made one of his frequent appearances at that point, volunteering at once to take Stacy's letter to the wall-box which—a hundred years ago—the two girls had noticed opposite his vicarage. Stacy told him briskly that they would have tea ready when he came back, and saw to it that Agatha supplied what help she could, which wasn't much, in the getting of that tea.

"Stacy," Agatha confessed humbly, "I don't seem to know *anything*."

"Oh, you'll soon learn!" Stacy comforted her briskly. "… No, *no*, Agatha! You *must* heat the pot before you put in the tea."

Since people in their twenties cannot mourn for ever, tea was quite a cheerful meal, in a subdued way; and the excellence of Stacy's thin bread and butter evoked much praise. And then Roger had to depart again, sorely against his will, to write a sermon; and the girls cleared away and washed up, and Agatha was heartened to find that the second time was distinctly easier than the first. She knew now where certain things were kept; she found that it was pleasant to see cups emerging from very hot water in a state of shining cleanliness.

"Stacy," she said suddenly, pausing as she turned to take a dry towel from the rack, "I think we could be quite happy, just you and I, without any servants at all: if only you wouldn't mind my being very slow and stupid while you taught me about things."

"You'd soon get tired of it, all day long," Stacy assured her rather shortly.

"I suppose this *would* be rather a big house to manage without any one," Agatha owned, looking wistfully about her.

Stacy only nodded. She did not know what to say. Agatha was evidently taking it for granted, as a matter of course, that she would go on living where she was, indefinitely.

"Won't you find this house too big?" was all that Stacy could bring herself to say after a short pause.

"Oh, but it's my *home*, Stacy!" Agatha cried, very much distressed. "I *couldn't* give it up! Why, darling Father chose it, and loved it, and it's—it's all full of him, everywhere. Besides, why should I?"

Stacy could only murmur again something about its being "so big."

"But you will come and live with me, of course!" Agatha pleaded earnestly. "Oh, Stacy, you *must*! That was the very first thing I thought of, when I could think of anything at all except Father. And, though I'm terribly sorry, of course, about your poor old ladies, it is wonderful that you are free now, and there's no reason for you ever to go away again. ... Stacy, you *will*? I'm sure we should be so happy together."

"I'm sure we should," Stacy murmured, in a lower voice still, without looking at the eager appealing face. Those piles and piles of business envelopes rose up before her mind's eye like a wall. She could not imagine it possible that Agatha would ever be able to keep on this large and expensive house, even if

"You will come and live with me, of course!"

they managed for themselves as much as possible, only having such servants as proved absolutely necessary. She looked out of the window at the lovely garden, and wondered how many gardeners were required to keep it in such perfect order. and how much wages they were all paid.

For the moment, of course, she could manage easily enough; and it would be good for Agatha to learn her way about her own house, and find out what ought to be done with her own belongings. For two or three picnic days they lived a hand-to-mouth and quite pleasant life; and then the final blow fell.

It came in the least likely manner possible, with the arrival of Lady Marjorie Clay from Scotland: the kindest of the kind, only eager to do anything and everything in her power, mingling her tears with Agatha's at their first meeting, but very soon brisk and energetic and business-like.

"I wouldn't let Toby come in till we'd got *this* over, dear. But I'll go and fetch him now; and he'll see to all your tiresome business affairs, and you'll have no more trouble."

"Toby" was not at all what might have been expected. He was her husband, the great Sir Tobias Clay, a very silent little keen-eyed man who was called Mr. Justice Clay and addressed as Judge. He said little or nothing when he shook hands with Agatha, merely asked for keys, called for Roger Blount (who was, as usual, somewhere in the near neighbourhood), and shut the two of them into the study. And there they stayed for an immense time, an occasional raised voice being heard at the telephone; and when they came out, the puzzle of Agatha's affairs had been unravelled to the last knot: a very sorry puzzle indeed.

The famous and attractive and wonderful Sir Humphrey Phayre had been spending money like water ever since Agatha left school; and every penny was gone. He might have lived comfortably enough, though not with splendour, on his quite comfortable income; but he preferred splendour, and he had spent capital as well as income on it. There was nothing left for Agatha at all, except her personal possessions and an enormous sheaf of unpaid bills. Even the house, which she had believed to be her own for ever, had never been paid for: only taken on a lease, of which one instalment had been paid. Sir Tobias looked indeed like a hanging judge (as some people called him) when he came out from that long examination, but he was very gentle with Agatha. He never mentioned her father to her at all; perhaps he could not trust himself to do so. He only explained that, instead of being rich, she was poor: even more than poor—penniless.

Agatha had borne a great deal in the last few days, and she hardly seemed to realize what all this meant. Her only comment made Lady Marjorie turn away sharply and feel for her handkerchief, while the judge's thick eyebrows closed right down over his keen eyes.

"Oh, I am so glad Father did not have to know all this; he would have hated so to be poor!"

There was one person present whose expression differed astonishingly from all the others, for it was one of unmixed pleasure. As Roger Blount made a quick step forward, Lady Marjorie caught her husband by one hand and Stacy by the other, and dragged them impetuously into the drawing-room.

"But I had not finished …" the judge protested, aggrieved.

"There is only one proper person to finish all this; and he's doing it now, a great deal better than you could, Toby, darling!" said Lady Marjorie. "The absolute end of all, you see, is going to be the only proper one: 'And so they lived happy ever after.'"

CHAPTER XV

THE POSTSCRIPT

AGATHA refused to leave the home that was not really hers any more, though Lady Marjorie was only too urgent, wanting to carry her away, there and then, for a visit of indefinite length. That most kind chatterer was really distressed about it; but her Toby, the only person capable of doing so, silenced her.

"She hasn't taken in her position yet. Leave her in peace with that very capable friend of hers, till she has had time to pull herself together."

"I'd love to have them *both*," said Lady Marjorie, almost in tears. "And Stacy could stay till she gets another job, and Agatha till she marries Roger. I'd *love* to run the wedding!"

The Judge merely remarked that they would be late for dinner; and Lady Marjorie got meekly into the car without another word and was driven away.

Agatha and Stacy started housekeeping in the large house that needed so many servants; and Agatha learned much, but most of all she learned her own incompetence. There was practically nothing that she could do without instruction, from making a bed to frying an egg. She watched Stacy going rapidly about her work with the sureness of experience, and her sense of ignorance and humiliation grew from hour to hour.

"If *only* I'd been taught like you, Stacy!" was her constant cry.

"You're learning," said Stacy, as encouragingly as was consistent with truth. For, as a matter of fact, Agatha was a slow learner; and at twenty-one, without ever previously having to do a hand's turn for oneself, household tasks appear mountainously difficult. She had at least, however, two great merits: she never resented correction, and she was unfailingly persevering.

"You see, I *must* learn, Stacy. I shall have to do so much in the house when I am married."

"Yes," said Stacy briefly. She had seen that for some time, and she knew the difficulties a great deal better than Agatha did. Roger Blount's vicarage was enormous. His income was three hundred a year, and Agatha had not a penny; and she was not at all the type that combats successfully with such people as his Mrs. Price. In the secret depths of her mind, Stacy seriously doubted whether they would be able to afford even that unattractive lady; and she could not faintly imagine Agatha doing the permanent work of a general servant in her own home. Needless to say, Stacy herself would love nothing better than to live with them and take most of the work on her own shoulders; but she could not do absolutely without money, and it seemed unlikely that they could afford to give her more than a microscopic salary.

In the meantime, they did not know from day to day when they might be turned out of the house that was no longer Agatha's. Even the furniture, it proved, was unpaid for; and Stacy had everlastingly at the back of her mind that large debt that was already owing to Lady Marjorie for the payment of the servants' wages. The present position was horrible, but the future was worse still. She put it out of her mind as far as possible and worked with all her might, watching meanwhile the weeds growing luxuriantly everywhere in the beautiful untended garden. She had quite enough on her hands as it was, without attending to anything outside the house.

Since they were so young, there were many times when all these anxieties could be forgotten, and they could thoroughly enjoy sharing work in each other's company. But Agatha was rapidly beginning to understand her painful position, and little things brought it home to her. … There was, for instance, the day when she light-heartedly insisted on making a cake for tea.

"No, don't tell me anything, Stacy! I've watched you so often, and I ought to do it by myself; I shall have to, presently."

Stacy quite agreed, but she walked out of the kitchen with a doubtful mind. There were so many things to remember, and Agatha was apt to get flustered and to forget. It was difficult to stay away, wondering what was happening. It was an immense relief when tones of triumph summoned her to the kitchen.

"Stacy, I've done it! Doesn't it look *lovely*!"

"Splendid!" Stacy praised her with warmth and relief, trying not to look at anything else but the cake, hot and golden before her. For Agatha had not yet learned to tidy up as she went, and the kitchen looked as if a battalion of untaught cooks had been making their first attempt at cake-making. But she would not for the world have damped the first joy of the amateur confectioner.

"Look, Roger! I made it all by myself. Stacy wasn't even in the kitchen!" Agatha cried to him gloriously, when he made his usual afternoon appearance. And naturally he thought her the eighth wonder of the world, and told her so at great length, Stacy tactfully failing to arrive for several minutes.

The tea was poured. The cake was cut. Roger, his adoring eyes fixed on Agatha, accepted a large slice with reverence.

"It's a little—damp inside, I'm afraid," said Agatha, her bright face falling.

"I like it damp," said Roger hastily.

"Cakes really should not be cut till the next day," Stacy assured her with equal haste.

"Oh, is *that* it?" said Agatha, relieved. "But isn't it rather—sticky?"

"It's apt to be, when you cut it hot," said Stacy.

Which, of course, is the case, as all cooks know. But even so, no cake should have a liquid inside.

"I expect you had the oven too hot," Stacy comforted the woebegone cake-maker.

"It *was* very hot—and I was so afraid of burning," Agatha almost sobbed.

"It isn't burnt in the least. It's a magnificent cake!" said Roger, eating valiantly.

Agatha was in such woe, after he left, that Stacy mercifully omitted to mention other flaws in her cookery: gritty currants that had not been cleaned, dark unpleasant spots of baking-powder, and large lumps of candied peel that should have been delicate shreds. Agatha was very chastened all that evening, and in the morning she came down with red-rimmed eyes.

"What *is* the matter?" Stacy inquired, alarmed.

"Oh, Stacy, I oughtn't to marry Roger at all! I don't know anything; and we can't afford proper servants; and I should make him *so* uncomfortable!"

Agatha wept freely; and Stacy, trying to comfort, was in the difficult position of knowing perfectly well that all these statements were true. The position really was extremely tragic.

"Do you think," Agatha asked, when she had quieted down and dried her eyes, "that I could go to your College, Stacy, and learn how to do things properly?"

"Lots of girls do, when they are going to be married," said Stacy, looking the other way.

"Do you think they could ever teach any one as old and stupid as I am?"

"Of course they could!" Stacy cried quickly. "There are people there much older than you, Agatha. And you're *not* stupid; you're only quite new to it all."

"Is it—very expensive?" Agatha asked timidly.

"Well, yes. Forty pounds a term," Stacy reluctantly owned.

"Forty pounds! And how many terms?" cried the girl whose dress allowance had been a hundred and fifty.

"Three," said Stacy briefly, still looking away. She could not bear to see the distressed hopelessness that, she knew, was creeping over the face gazing at her.

The rest of that day was most depressing; but Agatha appeared next morning bright-eyed and hopeful.

"Stacy, I know what I can do! I can sell my jewellery!"

"I suppose it is worth a great deal?" said Stacy, temporizing.

"Oh, I know Father paid ever so much for my string of pearls; and there are some rings that belonged to my mother; and that big Indian necklace …"

She would have to know the truth sometime. Stacy summoned up all her courage, and told it then and there.

"Agatha … you know your father left a good many debts behind him. I don't know … whether you will be allowed to keep expensive things like those …"

"But they're *mine*!" Agatha cried frantically.

"Yes. But the Judge said, as you are not twenty-one yet, they really belonged to your father. And, anyhow …" said Stacy, looking at her with sad but honest eyes.

"You mean," said Agatha after a minute, "that I ought not to keep things that would pay off some of the debts? … Yes; I see. … Of course not."

Her tears began to fall again, and Stacy could think of nothing comforting to say. She was quite glad to hear the postman's ring and go to fetch the letters. Those dreadful long envelopes had almost stopped coming now, and to-day there were none, only two, both addressed to herself. One had the Upper Galting postmark. The other was in Miss Pim's small, firm, characteristic writing, and Stacy tore this open with flushing cheeks. She had written at once, of course, to explain why she had left her first post, and she had had no answer. … She stood quite still, her colour fading away into whiteness.

The very temperamental cook of the Dorset school had renewed her engagement and married with next to no notice. The headmistress had written at once to Miss Pim asking if

Miss Wayland, whom she had liked so much, was still at liberty. If so, could she come, according to their previous arrangement of salary and so on, in about a fortnight's time?

Could Stacy accept? She could not; for how was it possible to leave Agatha in all her trouble and forlornness?

She stood quite still for a long time feeling rather cold, and then turned the page and read that Miss Pim was staying in London and would be glad to put her up for a night to talk things over. What an honourable invitation! and how equally impossible to accept. ... Besides, there was nothing *to* talk over. As long as Agatha wanted her, it was Stacy's privilege and duty to stand by her. ... No! Those fine buildings and magnificent grounds were not for her! It might be possible, she thought a little wildly, to find some job—daily cooking, for instance—where they could live together on what she earned.

Being Stacy, she thought suddenly of Mrs. Blott, and laughed instead of crying at the idea of her turning into a daily charlady. And then, feeling almost herself again, she opened the other envelope, and had hardly glanced at its contents when a honking sound in the drive announced Lady Marjorie and her Toby. As a matter of fact, she was an almost daily visitor, bringing fruit and all manner of good things; but he, as was natural, came but seldom.

"Well, Stacy, my dear, and what's that legal-looking letter, pray?"

"It sounds rather stupid, and I don't know what they mean. They wrote before," Stacy explained.

"Toby will tell you all about it," said Lady Marjorie blithely, passing it on without looking at it. "Where's Agatha? In the drawing-room? No, don't come!"

"This firm has written to you before, I understand?" said the Judge, looking up over his spectacles in the manner that had terrified many a criminal; but Stacy, feeling innocent, was not afraid of him at all. She explained, and produced the earlier letter from Mr. Harbinger, and told how she had answered.

"Well, you will have to see them at once," said the Judge in his quiet voice.

"Go to London?" Stacy cried, aghast.

"You can hardly expect them to come here, can you?" said the Judge, with his little dry smile. "There is evidently some doubtful point which needs discussion. ... Will you please tell me again all the details of your leaving Upper Galting?"

Which Stacy did, feeling rather bewildered. All that was, of course, over and done with. She could not imagine any possible reason why Mr. Harbinger should ever want to see her again.

"You were alone in the house, you say, when the younger Miss Postgate died?"

"Yes ... No!" said Stacy, suddenly recollecting. "The charwoman had sent her little boy to say that she was ill and could not come; and I had asked him in and given him some breakfast."

"Ah!" said the Judge gently, looking out of the hall door. "Well, you must be sure to mention that."

"I ... I suppose I oughtn't to have done it, because I was never allowed to have any one in," said Stacy, flushing. "But he's a cripple; and he was so tired with waiting. ... Do you think it was very wrong of me?"

"I think," said the Judge surprisingly, "that it may have been the wisest thing you ever did."

"Do *you* know why they want me, and what they mean?" Stacy challenged him point-blank.

The Judge did not answer her. Instead, he spoke to Lady Marjorie, just emerging from the drawing-room with a distressful face.

"Marjorie, my dear, we must shut this house up and take Agatha back with us."

"Just what I have always said! But she won't hear of it," cried Lady Marjorie.

"I think she will now," said the Judge, gently smiling. "She cannot possibly stay here alone; and Stacy has to go unexpectedly to London."

Upper Galting looked very much like itself: dusty, that is, and sun-baked, and dingy, with a stale flavour in the air suggesting that several hundred other people had breathed it first. Stacy was glad that she had not to go down St. Philibert's Terrace. She stopped at the house at the corner, and rang the bell near that brass plate that she had seen so often without noticing it. ... Yes. Mr. Harbinger was in, and was expecting her. If she would step this way. ...

It wasn't so terrible a solicitor's office as the grim room that belonged to Mr. Phipps; and Mr. Harbinger himself was very different indeed from the person who had always reminded her of Mr. Murdstone. Stacy was surprised, in fact, to remember that she had thought him grim-looking at their first meeting—a hundred years ago?—when she had admitted him for his interview with poor Miss Georgie. He reminded her of that at once.

"My errand then, Miss Wayland, was partly connected with you."

"With *me*?" Stacy repeated, staring at him in astonishment. (He really had very nice kind eyes, and his smile was a real smile.)

"Yes. I don't think you realize your own importance in this rather difficult business; you are, in fact, the only person who can tell us what we want to know."

"I'll tell you anything I can, of course," said Stacy.

"Tell me everything, then—even small details that you might not think important—about your return from your holiday."

He reminded her of that at once.

Stacy thought for a minute, and began. She told how she had returned, and rung, and waited to be let in; and then had found the door open, and had gone straight upstairs to bed, supposing that Miss Willie and Miss Georgie were unexpectedly out, as there was no light anywhere in the house. How she had overslept in the morning and run downstairs in dismay, and gone up with hot water and found first Miss Georgie obviously very ill and then Miss Willie dead.

He interrupted her there.

"You are sure of that?"

"Oh, yes; *quite* sure," said Stacy, with a little shiver of reminiscent horror. Then, remembering the Judge's injunctions, she told of Billy Blott, and how she had let him in and run downstairs to get him some breakfast after he had gone round to the doctor for her. And, when she came up again, how he was looking thoroughly frightened, and told her that "the lydy upstairs" had been calling for her. And she had run up again, and found ...

Stacy choked suddenly.

"Yes, I quite understand," said Mr. Harbinger quickly. "That was several minutes before the doctor came?"

"I don't know how long it was," said Stacy, very pale. "It seemed *years*."

Mr. Harbinger sat looking at her, saying nothing for a little while. When he spoke he asked a strange question.

"This cripple child, is he quite bright mentally?"

"Oh, *yes*!"

"How old?"

"Seven."

"Could you take me to see him? Does he live near?"

Only five minutes away, Stacy told him; and there was no fear that poor Billy would be out—he had to stay by himself all the long and weary day until his mother returned after her day's work. "It isn't safe for him without some one to take him over the crossings," Stacy explained sadly and earnestly.

"Did you do that sometimes?" Mr. Harbinger asked her suddenly.

"Oh, I took him out now and then," Stacy admitted, rather pink.

Upper Galting seemed, oddly, to have improved since she arrived there half an hour before. Perhaps the sun had come out. Perhaps, with some one to talk to as she walked, she did not notice its suburban deficiencies. At any rate, the short walk to Mrs. Blott's street had never seemed so short before; but what ages it appeared since she had last climbed those steep and unattractive stairs! and how long since that sharp little piping voice answered her knock.

"Come in! ... Oh, it's *Miss Cook*!"

Billy, forgetting his crutches, had stumbled anyhow across the floor and was clasping her round the knees.

"He always calls me that," Stacy explained, rather pink and confused. "Billy, I've brought a gentleman to see you. He wants to ask ..."

There were only two chairs in the room. Mr. Harbinger sat down on the one that had a broken back, and took Billy on his knee.

"Look here, old man! If you can tell me what I want to know, it will do a lot of good for your Miss Cook. And you'd like to help her, wouldn't you?"

Suspicion faded from Billy's face, and his sharp voice was resolute.

"Rah-ver!" he said. "I'd do *anyfing* for Miss Cook. She's been good to me, she has."

He told his side of the story with all the alertness of the quick-brained London child. How Mum's legs had been too bad for her to get up, and he had gone Sat'day, and Sunday, and Monday to tell the lydies that she couldn't come, and hadn't been able to make no one hear. But on Monday, after a bit, Miss Cook, *she* come, and told him the lydies was bad and he must go for the doctor. And when he come back, she told him to come in—what he'd never done afore—and wait while she got him some brekfuss, like.

"So you waited in the hall until she came back with the breakfast?"

Billy gave a gasp and turned a guilty pink. Stacy looked at him in surprise; for she had found him where she had left him, and it had never occurred to her that he had wandered elsewhere during her absence. True, she had wondered, for one alarming moment, whether he had pocketed any of the few pocketable things in the hall; and then had been ashamed of herself, and remembered the perfect honesty of Mrs. Blott, and had dismissed the unpleasant suspicion from her mind.

"What did you do, Billy, while Miss Cook was in the kitchen?" Mr. Harbinger asked.

Billy choked, and swallowed hard.

"We shall not be angry with you. We only want to know. Remember, it may mean a lot to Miss Cook."

"I—I went up them stairs," Billy murmured with hanging head.

"Yes?"

"I went into the front room …"

"Yes?"

"The lydy there—she was a stiff 'un."

"Are you sure about that?"

"Wishermaydie!" said Billy rapidly. "I've seen stiff 'uns afore—I have."

"And then?"

"I come out—quick."

"Yes?"

"Juss as I shut the door, the uvver door opened and the uvver lydy called out, in a norful voice, 'I want Anastasia!'— That's Miss Cook," Billy explained. "She allers called her that. Then she shut the door again, and I heard her go kerflump!"

Stacy, with a short, sharp shiver, remembered how she had found poor Miss Georgie lying face downwards on the floor.

"And then you came down again?"

"Not arf, I didn't!" Billy confirmed with energetic nods. "And Miss Cook, she came up, and she guv me tea and bread and syrup …"

Mr. Harbinger put him down gently and stood up.

"Not arf, I didn't!" Billy confirmed.

"You're a fine boy, Billy. You've done more for your Miss Cook than you can understand," he said. "Now, Miss Cook …" He smiled at her.

"She's *my* Miss Cook, not yours!" Billy told him very sharply. "Nobody don't call her that 'cept me! *You* can call her An-as-tas-ia."

"Perhaps I will some day—if she will let me," said Mr. Harbinger. "No, she can't wait to take you out to-day; we have to do some important business at once. Look! That's for your mother when she comes in, and that's for you."

"Hi, Mister! 'Tain't a penny; it's a arf a cround!" Billy told him shrilly.

"Clever boy," said Mr. Harbinger, and stood smiling while Stacy took her leave, promising to come again some time.

They walked back in perfect silence to his office; and now the dull streets seemed to be going wildly round and round, from Stacy's point of view. The whole thing was a dark mystery, and she could see no reason in it at all; but presumably Mr. Harbinger could, or he would not have smiled quietly to himself as he went along.

"Now!" he said at last when they were sitting opposite each other again. "You don't understand any of this, do you?"

Stacy shook her bewildered head.

"That day when I went to see Miss Georgie—you remember?"

There was no reason why Stacy should have turned pink at the remembrance, but she did.

"She sent for me to add a codicil to her will—a sort of postscript."

Stacy nodded vaguely. She knew that.

"She and her sister had made exactly similar wills, years before, each leaving everything to the other. It must have been some strange presentiment which made Miss Georgie suddenly wonder what would happen if they died more or less at the same time, before the survivor could make a fresh will. They had only one relation: a very distant cousin whom they both disliked.—Don't you want to know what the codicil said?"

Stacy did not speak.

"It was very short. 'In case my sister dies before me, I leave everything I have to Anastasia Wayland, who has always been so kind to me.'"

"I ... never did anything," Stacy sobbed, winking hard.

Mr. Harbinger's tone became suddenly quite stiff and legal, which was a great help.

"You see our difficulty? The ladies died within such a short time of each other that it was impossible for even the doctor to decide which death occurred first. Your unsupported evidence was naturally valueless, especially as you were the person who would benefit. Your friend Billy Blott has saved the situation—a bright little boy, as you say."

Stacy had dried her eyes by this time and recovered her voice.

"Yes?" she said, trying to be stiff and legal too.

"If Miss Georgiana had died first, Miss Wilhelmina would have been her heir. As it is, Miss Georgiana lived just long enough to inherit her sister's property. And it now all becomes yours."

"Not Miss Willie's too?" Stacy cried. "Oh, I'm *sure* she wouldn't have liked that!"

Mr. Harbinger, smiling very suddenly and irrepressibly, became unlegal again.

"There's no help for that, I'm afraid. ... Not afraid; *sure*.— Don't you want to know the amount of your inheritance?"

Stacy looked up, bright-eyed. There was so much that she could do with even a little money! and she had never had the spending of anything to speak of in her life.

"Death duties will cut it down very much, of course; but you should have certainly not less than fifteen thousand pounds."

"*What?*" Stacy cried in a voice very unlike the usual decorous tones of a solicitor's office. "But I thought they were poor!"

"So, possibly," said Mr. Harbinger, "did Miss Georgie. Her sister was a very clever manager."

He mercifully lapsed into silence, for Stacy's head was going round again. It was she who spoke again, after several minutes.

"Will it be my very own; to do exactly as I like with?"

"To do exactly as you like with," Mr. Harbinger assured her gravely.

"Can I, please, give half of it away to somebody?"

"If you wish to do so, certainly. But you really ought to think it well over before taking so serious a step."

"I don't want to think; I *know*!" cried Stacy, all joy and eagerness and impatience. "Oh, you'll arrange it for me, won't you? I don't want her to know where it comes from—*ever*. I want her to think that her father left it to her. Oh, you *can* do that for me, can't you?"

Mr. Harbinger hesitated a little. Then he said: "If you really wish it, of course I can."

CHAPTER XVI

THE sunny side of Regent Street on a fine summer morning is a cheerful place, full of thrills for the feminine person; but it is unlikely that Stacy, gazing into one after another of those too alluring shops, met any face so bright as her own. She had money in her pocket; for Mr. Harbinger had delicately suggested that this might be a convenience, as she was unlikely to receive her legacy for some time to come. She was staying with Miss Pim for a couple of nights, and they had had the most thrilling conversation on the evening before, going over Stacy's interests past, present, and future. And Miss Pim had been unbelievably human, even calling her "Stacy" in the most natural manner, whereas heretofore she had always seemed unaware of any name except Miss Wayland. She had taken the kindest interest in the vexed question of Agatha; and in this connection a miracle had happened, for there was actually an unfilled place in next term's College list. Such a thing had, surely, never happened before, for there was usually a waiting-list of alarming length; but a prospective student had dropped out suddenly owing to a very bad motor accident, and all the rest of the waiting-list had already found other temporary occupations. So Agatha should go to College and learn how to keep her house when she married; and she should find, to her relief and surprise, that when all those terrible debts were paid she still had a comfortable little nest-egg left; and she would never, as long as she lived, know who was at the bottom of this; and she and her Roger would live happily ever afterwards. And Stacy, in her different way, would do the same, enjoying her Dorset school more than she could have found possible without her intervening time at Upper Galting. And she would be able to do all sorts of delightful things in the holidays, because, of course, she thought wisely, a married Agatha wouldn't want her every time. And if she fell ill or anything, or lost her job, there would be no need to worry, because she also would have a comfortable nest-egg on which, like the Irishman, she could take her stand in her old age.

How extraordinarily kind, Stacy thought glowingly, every one had been to her! She had always suspected Miss Pim of being a real friend underneath her alarming exterior, and now she knew it to be true. Poor dear Miss Georgie had repaid a thousandfold all those small kindnesses that had been shown her whenever possible. Even Mr. Harbinger, practically a stranger—(and a lawyer to boot; and Stacy had no reason to love lawyers)—had taken the most immense pains to explain and be helpful, even to the point of carefully assuring himself that Stacy had friends to stay with in London.

"Because I am sure," he had incredibly observed, "my mother would be delighted to put you up; and I should like you to meet her."

Stacy was polite, in an astonished way, about that; but naturally she would immensely rather stay with Miss Pim, though she did not put it so brutally. Mr. Harbinger really seemed quite sorry that she was already arranged for; and he seemed also to think that it might be necessary for him and Stacy to meet more than once over details of her inheritance, and in that case—he brought in his mother again, and seemed to intend the suggestion to be taken seriously. ... He had, in fact, been very kind indeed.

Waking up from a long meditation over all this, Stacy found herself standing with her unseeing eyes glued to a window filled with handbags of the most entrancing kinds and varieties—rather dear; but she needn't worry about that now! It seemed to her that the most attractive occupation for the next few minutes would be to go in and buy something that she didn't really need at all, just for the unaccustomed pleasure of spending money. So in she went, and gloated for a good many minutes over the bewildering choice before her; and finally, being Stacy, suddenly bought a fascinating guinea bag with a zip-fastener, and had it packed and sent off to Aunt Monica—poor Aunt Monica, who had all her money doled out to her shilling by shilling, and never could buy anything that wasn't strictly necessary. Stacy gave a sudden gurgle, to the great astonishment of the shop-lady, at the thought of Mr. Phipps's face of baffled surprise and displeasure, and the practical certainty of his pointing out that "the price of that bag, Monica, would have paid for nearly half a ton of coal."

Still full of this merry conceit, Stacy walked out of the shop and collided with some one walking fast along the pavement.

"I'm so sorry …"

"Oh, I beg your pardon—*Stacy!*"

"Janet! Oh, do come and shop with me!"

"Sorry. I can't. I've got a business appointment."

"Let me walk with you, then," said Stacy, disappointed, but unwilling to part like this. For one thing, she had never (and it had always lain on her conscience) done anything for Janet in return for that tea, when she had felt it her duty to eat such very heavy scones and refuse sugar-cakes. Now she could indeed return chicken for chicken, with a vengeance!

Janet said ungraciously that she was in a hurry, and would have to take the next 44 bus that came along. But Stacy, not to be put off, walked rapidly beside her.

"Aren't these your office hours?"

"I've left my uncle's office," said Janet shortly.

"But I thought you liked it so much?"

"All business men are feeling the present depression," said Janet in her informing, superior fashion. "My uncle had to reduce his staff, and I was the latest joined."

"Oh, I'm sorry," said Stacy, hoping that it was not unkind to wonder if it was personal unpopularity as well as being a junior that had made Janet's uncle forget the claims of kinship.

"I'm just going to apply for another post now," Janet told her. "Very much pleasanter; some of the clerks *were* rather common. Look!"

She held out a newspaper cutting, and Stacy read it with some difficulty; for it is not easy to read small print while

Stacy read it.

walking rapidly along Regent Street in the middle of the morning.

"'—Retired Vice-Admiral requires Lady Secretary, immediately. Duties light, hours short, salary generous. Knowledge of typewriting and shorthand not essential. Apply between 12 and 1, 19 Patmore Square, S.W.'"

"Here's my bus," said Janet.

"Do let me come too," said Stacy.

"Oh, if you like, of course. I don't suppose I shall be kept there very long."

Janet's tone implied that any retired vice-admiral would naturally engage her at sight.

"Then you'll come and lunch with me," said Stacy eagerly.

"Oh!" Janet stared a little. "If you're sure that you …"

"Yes, I can quite well afford it," Stacy ended for her cheerfully, and Janet had the grace to blush slightly. She eyed Stacy, sitting by her in the bus, with critical side-glances, and undoubtedly she found her shabby. But Stacy, for her part, had not failed to notice that Janet herself was not so trig as usual. One shoe had a downtrodden heel; and her hat had been obviously retrimmed with a fresh ribbon, which just didn't match it. She was looking round condescendingly at other inhabitants of the bus, as if wondering whether she had here any rivals to fear. There was a pale efficient-looking girl in black; there was an elderly woman with an anxious lined face; there was a pert little minx about five foot tall—the sort of person whom not even Janet would find it easy to snub. …

"Patmore Square!" said the conductor.

Janet stepped nimbly off the bus, with Stacy at her heels; and the girl in black, the elderly woman, and the little minx followed apace, all of them, it was now quite obvious, caught as Janet had been by that alluring advertisement. She looked a little annoyed about this, saying to Stacy, in a voice intentionally unlowered:

"Of course, though typing and shorthand are not *essential*, it is a very great advantage to have been properly trained in that way. … I think it's this corner."

As she turned it the little minx shot past her, with a giggle and impudent side glance that were also intentionally obvious. The elderly woman and the girl in black were quickening their footsteps behind; and Janet, squaring her elbows a little, did the same. …

And paused suddenly; and Stacy gave a little gasp. She had never seen such a sight in her life.

As London Squares go, Patmore Square was small: possibly fifty houses. Like many other London Squares, it was not square at all, but a sort of irregular oblong, with a forlorn railed-in patch of grass and trees taking up the middle of it; and this was the only part of it that was not blocked and choked with women. A house in a corner, obviously Number Nineteen, had its invisible steps completely covered with them, fighting their way up and down. All along the pavement, all along the roadway, they pressed and thronged upon each other: some angry, some hopeful, some hopeless, all anxious and determined—and somewhere near at hand a church clock was striking twelve.

The little minx was pushing and thrusting her way in front of earlier comers; and at that sight Janet recovered herself, squared shoulders as well as elbows, and stepped stoutly forward, Stacy perforce accompanying her, because it was absolutely impossible to turn back. It was a most horrible situation. The only mercy was that there was some other outlet to the Square at the far end—nobody was coming back. If they had done that, Stacy thought with horror, some of them *must* have been killed.

She was glad that the little minx had been brought up short against a broad-shouldered woman about six foot high; she was sorry for a white-faced creature who turned faint and wanted to get out of the crush, and couldn't by any means do it. There were hateful things being said all around; there were much worse things that were only looked. Slowly, slowly the surging mass fought its way towards that house in the corner; and Stacy cast a hasty glance over her shoulder, and as hastily looked in front again. The crowd behind was almost as thick as the crowd before: a breath-taking vision ...

It occurred to her, suddenly, that no one was being let into Number Nineteen at all.

Janet did not appear to have noticed this; she was wholly occupied in fighting her way along, so as to gain if possible a little space where any appeared for a moment; but Stacy had now no doubt about it at all. People surged up the steps, looked at some sort of notice fastened on the door, and surged down again, looking furious or tearful as the case might be. As a sudden rush from behind lifted Stacy clear off her feet for a moment and carried her to the bottom step, she heard a sobbing voice uplifted from the girl just moving off it. "Oh, it's a shame! a wicked, cruel *shame*!"

"Come along!" said Janet suddenly, clutching her by the hand. She had just come down from the door; she looked extraordinarily white, and her eyes stared. Together, in silence, they fought their way out to the farther entrance of the square and turned down the nearest side-street that looked quiet.

"I'm afraid the—the post was already filled?" Stacy ventured at last, for Janet was merely walking along with her head down, as if she saw and heard nothing. Hearing Stacy's voice, she started.

"Post? ... There *wasn't* any post!"

"No? ..."

"Didn't you read the notice?"

"I didn't get near enough," said Stacy.

Janet, staring in front of her, spoke in a queer loud voice that had no inflections.

"'Vice-Admiral Petersford has inserted NO advertisement, and requires NO secretary.'"

"But ..."

"Just a hoax!" said Janet in the same loud voice. "I suppose somebody thought it funny, or they had a grudge against the admiral, or some journalist thought it would make a good story." She spoke with a sudden passion: "Yes, that was it! Didn't you see those two men watching as we came out? Didn't you hear what they said?"

Stacy shook her head, more than half frightened; Janet looked so dreadfully unlike herself. "I did! Something about 'secretaries like sand on the seashore, and clerks twopence a dozen ...' I've lost my bag!"

She looked wildly round, made as if to go back, saw the steady stream of disappointed women pouring steadily out of the Square, and burst into tears.

"Stacy, I *must* find it! I haven't another penny in the world!"

"Oh, Janet! Was it much?"

A little of the old Janet came creeping back at that question, but the voice that answered shook woefully.

"Oh, not much! Only about—about seven shillings!"

It would never, never do, of course, to offer to refund that (now, to Stacy) inconsiderable sum, but there were ways and means. She only urged that they should go and get some luncheon at once; and Janet followed her meekly, perhaps the first time that she had ever done such a thing, certainly the only time that she did not find something captious to say about Stacy's going to a place of that sort. It wasn't, as London restaurants go, anything very palatial, but it was vastly superior to the place where Stacy had humbly eaten a tea of stodgy scones.

So shaken was Janet that it seemed at first as if she would be unable to eat, but she cheered up after soup, and by the arrival of sweets was sufficiently herself to observe it was odd how every place of this sort gave exactly the same choice! She made, in fact, a very satisfactory meal: only offering an odd suggestion as they came out.

"I ... don't want to go home just yet, Stacy. Let's go and sit in the park."

"All right," Stacy agreed; for Miss Pim had had a luncheon engagement that day and did not expect her back till tea-time. So in the park they sat, in a most unnatural silence which Stacy filled quite pleasurably to herself with a beautiful new scheme that had just come into her head. ... Mrs. Blott should go into a hospital and have her bad legs made into good legs; and Billy should go to some orthopædic place where proper treatment would turn him from a cripple into an ordinary walking and running boy; and Roger Blount's detestable Mrs. Price should be outed, and Mrs. Blott installed in her stead, with Billy growing and flourishing in the good Welsh air. (All of which, more or less, came to pass in due time, with conspicuous success.) So enthralled was Stacy by these enchanting visions, that only a very unexpected sound could have brought her rapidly back to what photographers call Present Day—the sound of a thick, heavy sob. Janet, the all-knowing and the self-sufficient, was crying her heart out.

"Janet, *dear*" (and it was the first time that Stacy had ever brought herself to say that), "what *is* the matter?"

"I must get a job!" Janet sobbed miserably. "Mother can't afford to keep me at home doing nothing. I used to give her ten shillings a week, you know; and it's *awful* to have no money of your own! And I've answered advertisements till I'm *sick*; and they don't answer; and I can't afford to advertise for myself; and I *must* get a job!"

And here even Stacy's new powers were at an end. She could, and did, sympathize most heartily. She could, and did, presently (when Janet had dried her eyes and thought she ought to go) insist on buying her a new bag, and see to it, secretly, that it contained more than seven shillings before changing hands. But she could not alter a condition of life where secretaries were as plentiful as sea sand, and clerks twopence a dozen.

She walked back very seriously towards tea and Miss Pim. But, after all, she had done all she could; and there was another delightful evening before her; and to-morrow she would see Agatha—and face Lady Marjorie without a constant dragging memory of that unpayable debt that would now be so soon paid off. ...

"Well, Stacy! A pleasant day?" said Miss Pim.

"No. Dreadful, most of it," said Stacy, drawing a long breath. "But, oh, Miss Pim, it's made me more glad than you can think that I'm—just me!"

Books to Treasure

Old favourites

E M CHANNON:
The Cinderella Girl
Expelled from St Madern's
A Fifth Form Martyr
Her Second Chance
The Honour of the House (eBook only)

E E COWPER (eBook only):
Camilla's Castle

SARAH DOUDNEY (eBook only):
Monksbury College
When We were Girls Together

EVELYN EVERETT-GREEN (eBook only):
Queen's Manor School

BESSIE MARCHANT (eBook only):
By Honour Bound
The Two New Girls

eBooks available for download from all Amazon sites
sales@bookdragonbooks.co.uk   www.bookdragonbooks.co.uk

DOROTHEA MOORE (eBook only unless specified):
Brenda of Beech House
Fen's First Term
A Plucky Schoolgirl
A Runaway Princess
Septima Schoolgirl
Séraphine-Di Goes to School
Tam of Tiffany's
Wanted: an English Girl (print & eBook)
The Wrenford Tradition (print & eBook)

EVELYN SMITH:
Seven Sisters at Queen Anne's (Queen Anne's 1)
Septima at School (Queen Anne's 2)
Phyllida in Form III (Queen Anne's 3)

Val Forrest in the Fifth (Myra Dakin's 1) (eBook only)
Milly in the Fifth (Myra Dakin's 2)

Biddy and Quilla
The First Fifth Form
Nicky of the Lower Fourth
The Small Sixth Form

ETHEL TALBOT:
The New Girl at the Priory

THEODORA WILSON WILSON (eBook only):
Founders of Wat End School

Lightning Source UK Ltd.
Milton Keynes UK
UKOW06f0111040316

269598UK00001B/22/P